Commanding Fire

Dallas Fire & Rescue
(Kindle Worlds)

Bestselling Author

Siera London

COMMANDING HEAT

Cover art by Fantasia Frog
Images licensed via DepositPhoto

Edited by Gayla Leath of Dark Dreams Editing

About This Book

On the run and alone, Victoria Currey has two weeks to rescue her father. Unfortunately, she wakes up in a hospital bed, with a sexy stranger whose voice she recognizes, and four days left. With no money and no one to turn to, how long does she have before she's captured again?

Firefighter, Trace Fletcher's organized life is turned upside down when he pulls an unconscious sleeping beauty from a fire. He knows he can't have her, but from the moment she turns those soft brown eyes on him, he never wants to let her go. The veiled fear lurking in their depths calls to his dark past and the life he left behind.

For Victoria, Trace is unlike any man she's ever met, and she has every intention of exploring the passion he commands until reality catches up to her. The heat between them rages out of control, but their passion comes at a price. When danger comes knocking, demanding payment, it's not just Victoria's life in peril, but the carefully constructed walls Trace has erected between his old life and new beginning.

Acknowledgements

Special thanks to Paige Tyler for creating the *Dallas Fire & Rescue* world filled with kick-butt heroines and sexy firefighters. I had a lot of fun letting my imagination run wild with Sleeping Beauty and Beauty and the Beast. Trace and Tori's story may be the end of the road for my Key West crew, so enjoy the magic carpet ride.

—To Fire Captain D. Austin, your input has been invaluable.

—To Carole, thank you for the French lesson.

—To my editor, Gayla Leath, you are the answer to my prayers.

—To Shannon Lester-Hayes, you have freed me to write and I can't thank you enough.

—To Michele, Angel, Xyla, LaQuette, and Tammy, you are my sounding board and my support network. You are all amazing ladies and I'm grateful for your friendship.

—As always, to Mr. Awesome, you are my romance of a lifetime.

—To Him who is able to keep us from falling, both now and forever, thank you, God.

Sincerely,
Siera

Chapter One

White light and a surge of intense heat filled the hallway a second before Victoria Currey was hurled through the air. The entire building, a two-story structure for senior citizens, vibrated. The sound of shattering glass panes began, one after the other in perfect concert, as flames leaped from open doors along the residential corridor. The force of the explosion slammed her back against the wall, where she crash-landed. Her body folded like a dry leaf propelled to the ground by a violent wind. Pain wrapped around her shoulders and slashed the length of her spine. As the horrendous sensation snaked down her legs, she held her breath until spots danced before her eyes. Her body demanding oxygen, she gasped in a deep inhale. Instantly, she regretted the action. Thick smoke, acrid and toxic, filled her throat. The burn traveled quickly to her chest making it difficult to expand her lungs.

She lay there, all too aware of the fire encroaching on her location.

Mustering her strength, she pressed soot-covered fingers against the tile and dragged herself upright from the floor.

"Dear heaven." The hot air had a sauna effect, making her light-headed. Tori couldn't pass out. She'd traveled for two days on the bus to reach her father. They both needed to get out of Key West to avoid capture again.

Flames burst into the hallway on her left. She watched as the blaze grew, branching in multiple directions, a ravenous blossom with an unlimited food supply. Fear shot through her, but she held the sob inside. She would probably die here, on the floor, defeated. Something crashed beyond the flames. Like a zipper released, the inferno wall separated and a big body clothed in a reflective suit emerged. A firefighter. His confident stride held an air of menace that seemed to command the scorching heat to abate. A mask with some type of breathing apparatus covered his face, but she could sense his eyes on her. Her torso collapsed on her extended arm. Without regard to pride or position, she called to him.

"Help me."

A huge arm caught her around the back, lifting her. Tori's curves filled the cradle he formed when he swept her off her feet, her body pressed against a chest double the size of her. Black clouds of smoke sandwiched them in. Her eyes burned, the heat had evaporated her tears. Charred stench surrounded them. As he navigated through darkened spaces, jostling her in his arms, she clenched her teeth against the stinging bite in her head. *Oh God, Daddy where are you?* She wouldn't survive if she lost him too.

She whimpered, clinging to her savior.

"I've got you," he said. His voice was dark and melodic. Her stomach fluttered, and she jerked at the unfamiliar tingle. "Be still now. Almost outside and you'll be safe."

After what seemed like an eternity, the warmth of the bright sunlight touched her skin. Hungry for oxygen, she tried to cough up the tar plugging her airways. Voices and moving bodies swarmed about her. She tried to raise her head, looking for her father's silvery mane.

"Try not to move. I'll get you to a gurney."

"Help..." she whispered as panic gripped her. She couldn't get a breath in.

Flailing, she grabbed at her throat. Her heart beat wildly in her chest. She was dying. She'd lost control of the cough. The more she tried to take in a full breath, the harder it became to get the toxic fumes out. "Help."

What would her father do when he discovered she'd died mere feet away from him? Her rescuer stilled, and then he tore off his face gear. Dark eyes, a rich cognac in color and softer than the angles of his face, regarded her.

3

"No, no," he repeated. "I need a gurney over here," he yelled. He cupped her cheek in his massive hand. "Stay with me."

Though just a whisper, she heard the catch in his throat, the anguish in his voice. Wanting to see his face, Tori forced her eyes to travel the arduous distance. Finally, their gazes met. His dark pools fixed on her. It was probably her imagination, but it was as if he cared beyond his call of duty, like he had a personal stake in her survival. He lowered her onto something hard, all the while maintaining eye contact.

"I won't let you go," he said. Determination flashed in his eyes.

She clawed at his jacket, digging her nails in the dense material to hold on. Desperation tore at her insides. The need to prolong the connection and deliver a final message had her clutching at this lifeline.

"Help...father," she tried to say, but the words were garbled to her own ears. She felt the rising tide of emotion, but the tears would never come. Her body fought to conserve the vital fluid. With her wrists pinned together in his hand, he issued commands. Tori latched onto the sound of his voice, taking the resonant tones into the chasm with her. She heard packages being ripped opened, and sirens that were fading into the distance. And she realized her pain had vanished.

"I'm losing her," someone bellowed.

She couldn't tell if it was her firefighter anymore. Added pressure squeezed her chest, but then it was gone.

"Protect...," she uttered with her last breath. Her lungs stiffened beneath her ribs, and then stopped the struggle to breathe. The feel of firm lips pressed against hers registered in her mind before the abyss yawned wide and sucked her into darkness.

❖

Why had she asked him to protect her? Trace Fletcher sat forward in the bedside chair. The plastic material groaned under his two-hundred-and-eighty-pound weight. His jeans slid across the seat cushion, damp with humidity even in the air-conditioned hospital room. It was the first week of May, and the Key West heat had driven the snowbirds back north. His three days off rotation from the Key West Old Town Firehouse had started yesterday. Normally, he spent Fridays at Hobo Alley with his hand wrapped around a cold beer. In the past six years, nothing had changed in his routine...until four days ago.

He stared at the woman he'd pulled from the blaze at the Island Life Senior Citizen's facility. The staff had taken to calling her Sleeping Beauty. Interestingly, the doctors thought her continued retreat in and out of consciousness had more to do with exhaustion than smoke inhalation. What kind of life had she lived before now? Rich sable waves hung loose over her shoulders. The grime had hidden flawless, sun bronzed skin. Her pert nose wiggled sometimes in her sleep. He thought it made her look a little mischievous. With that one uttered word - *protect*- she'd changed him, awakening an instinct he thought buried. How was she different from all the other women he'd met? He needed to know. He found himself wondering what kind of magic could they create together. But, she had to wake up for him to understand this supernatural pull she had over him. He reached for her hand. Briefly, he held her smaller hand in his large paw, willing her to open her eyes.

"Look at me, Beauty." Trace repeated this request every day. She didn't know it, though he'd told her more than once, they were running out of time. The department's competency training program required him to travel to Dallas Fire & Rescue Station 58 once a year. In seven days, he'd have to leave. She didn't owe him anything. He'd been doing his job when he'd saved her life, but he wanted to see her mocha-colored eyes beneath those impossibly long lashes again before he left for DF&R Station 58.

There was no room in his life for a woman. His job as a firefighter kept him busy. He didn't have the time for romance, which was a good thing. He found other ways to meet his needs, usually involving a hand puppet with a soapy center. Nope, a woman needed to be protected, and he'd failed in that department six years ago. Movement on the bed drew his attention. He performed a slow perusal of her curvy form, surveying for any changes from the last hour when he'd done the same. As always, his eyes settled on the old needle marks that ravaged the delicate skin in the fold of both her arms. Her small frame, unmoving, looked elegant and refined, not like that of a junkie. Unconsciousness was a safe haven of sorts. Maybe the universe had a hand in keeping him and Beauty protected. After seeing her arms, he'd expected her to show withdrawal symptoms. She was feisty. He remembered how she'd struggled in his arms. The nurses could use an extra set of hands if she were in an agitated state. He'd told himself that's why he came every day he could, staying until visiting hours ended.

She inhaled a deep breath and he came to his feet. He noticed she'd been doing that more often in the past eight hours. When he pulled her from the fire, she'd been barely conscious. Deprived of oxygen, the brain could conjure hallucinations. But, Trace had felt the urgency as she struggled to speak. Then she'd stopped breathing. He'd dropped to his knees beside her soot-covered body, tilted her head back, pinched her nose, and sealed his mouth to hers. Even with smoke clinging to her skin, she'd tasted sweet. How he remembered her delicate flavor, he didn't know. Approaching the bed, he brushed a finger over her cheek. The feel of her skin was soft, and his fingers tingled where they touched. He thought her eyelids flickered, but—maybe not.

"Open your eyes for me. Just once."

She'd been discovered without any identification and no one from the seniors' village remembered her visiting a resident. Her presence on the scene remained a mystery.

"Beauty," he said, now leaning over the bed rail in place. "When you wake up, I'll be gone."

He chuckled to himself. Why had he come back to see her every day? Because, he knew he would miss her. A woman that didn't know he existed. How pathetic was that? He needed to end this. What kind of guy needed to

8

end things with an unconscious woman? Since he'd been the one to pull her from the building, he thought of her as his responsibility.

"I can't." He paused. "I can't come back here. I'd hoped some family would show up to take care of you." Trace ran his fingers through the length of his hair, until the strands narrowed beneath a rubber band. Gosh, it was just as hard breaking things off with an unconscious woman. "Heck, I don't know how to do this."

That had been his problem before, he didn't know how to let go. Everything had to be ripped from his hands like a spoiled rotten kid. So, he'd learned not to connect, that way he wouldn't have to let go. He had his job and his crew. That would have to be enough.

He looked at the woman on the bed. He imagined her looking at him, grateful that he had honored her request. He'd kept her safe while she slept. *Protected*.

"I should go."

Trace turned and grabbed the book he'd been reading to her and the two empty Pepsi bottles. The third held room temperature liquid inside now. He'd drink it tomorrow. No, he wouldn't, because he wasn't coming back to see her.

Walk out the door, he told himself. He couldn't fill

his empty life by sitting at an unconscious stranger's bedside. He needed to leave. It was what he was best at these days.

He pulled the door open. Bells, ringing phones, and the mechanical hum of hospital equipment greeted him. He angled his head ready to look back, check on her one last time, but he stopped himself. *She's not your responsibility.* She was a job. The job was over.

"Tra...Trace," came a groggy voice from behind him.

At the soft flutter of his name, he spun around. Panic, wild and untamed, flared in her fathomless eyes. Trace stalked back to the bed, never taking his gaze off her. He transferred his crap to one hand, lowered the side rail, and sat beside her on the bed. Her hip touched his, and heat seeped through the layer of blankets into him. He didn't want her to be upset so soon after she'd awakened.

"Shh," he said.

She tore at the bedcovers. "I have to stop..." her voice stalled.

He gestured to the door. "You need something? A nurse?"

She stared at him. He got the feeling she was asking questions of herself and answering all the while holding his gaze. She had awoken in a panic, but also ready for action. She was a survivor. He liked that about her.

"Hey, hey," he said. His gentle hand at her cheek slowed her frantic movements. "What's wrong? What do you need?" Beauty's eyes, a soft brown, were focused on him. The vulnerability he saw as she searched his face for answers slay him. His pulse picked up speed. Desire, swift and hot, licked at his skin. He'd thought her beautiful before, but those rounded doe eyes with a slight lift at the corners sucked him in.

"Your name is Trace Fletcher."

"You could hear me…while you were unconscious?" His heart thumped against his chest. Trace leaned in close and took a deep inhale. Ah, he'd wanted this moment with her for what felt like an eternity. The scent of fresh melon, light and airy, assaulted him. Remembered sweetness tingled on his tongue, making him salivate. He never imagined that the aroma of a woman could enthrall him to the point of physical need.

Abruptly, her breath hitched. Dark eyes shot to his, and then her pupils dilated. "Every word."

Suddenly, every cell in his body snapped to attention at her soft soprano. She didn't seem alarmed, quite the opposite. What the hell had he said to her?

11

Chapter Two

Tori awoke with a churning stomach. Nausea crested, but she pressed one hand against her belly, squashing the sensation. The urge to act clawed through the haze in the forefront of her mind. She had to stay awake or she'd lose someone important. Who? Confused about her whereabouts, alarm bells sounded in her head. Who else would be taken away from her? His voice, the one that had been with her in the darkness, called to her. In her mind, she could see a bridge spanning the divide between darkness and light. This time, she moved toward it and grabbed ahold. She rode the deep, full-bodied notes back into a bright clearing. She opened her eyes for the briefest of moments and he was there.

"Trace?" He'd helped her. Wincing against the light, she closed her eyes.

"Right here," he said, taking her hand.

Memories began to surface. A marriage stipulation had been added to her trust. Her questions about her father's health that went unanswered. Discovering that her father had been relocated without her knowledge. The drugs she'd been given, her escape from the mansion, the pawn shop in Southwest DC where she'd left her pendant. There were other memories, too. Images were cutting through her addled brain, lightning strikes, each one jolting her back to life. The nursing home where Denton had hidden her father, the fire, her struggle to breathe, Trace's mouth on hers. Her mind went in reverse. Where was her father?

She slid her eyes open, this time nice and slow. Stark beige walls adorned with distressed wood-framed prints spaced equidistant around the room. Such was the sterile nature of hospitals. With a groan, she turned her head to the right. Full bloom red roses in a dark green vase sat on the cubby sink.

"Roses...you?" she whispered.

He gave a stiff nod. His coffee brown eyes that were hard a moment before, softened with an infusion of gold transforming them to a warm maple. He'd brought her flowers. The red ones were her favorite, too. The fact that he sought to surround her with beauty as she slept endeared him to her. The rest of the subdued decor was a physical queue to remain neutral, not too dire, and not too optimistic. A sober reminder that she needed to find her father before Denton found her.

"It was you who saved me, right?" Her voice sounded

rusty and unused. "My firefighter."

The man at her side shifted, his thigh brushed against hers. Her skin heated on contact. She took a long look at him. Six foot three, give or take a millimeter. Coal black hair pulled back from his forehead and gathered in a tie. She pressed her back against the pillows, angling her head. The shiny black mane reached past his shoulder blades. Eyes the color of a midnight sea under the moonlight, dark, yet iridescent, regarded her from beneath long lashes and heavy brows. A straight nose, too perfect for his hard jaw line, with a rounded tip was his only refined quality. Even his lips, full with a slight tint, twisted at the corner giving over to a fierce quality. He wore an army green t-shirt with khaki-colored cargos. Talk about *hi, ho, Silver, away*. He was a gorgeous warrior. His body was thick, muscled, and intimidating, but all that warm colored skin paid penance to his hulking frame.

"I'm a firefighter, among other things." She gave him a sideways glance, and he got the message to answer the question. "Yeah, it was me."

Trace tightened his hold on her hand. She might have imagined it, but it felt like he was stroking her skin, inside and out.

"You had to revive me. I remember..." she said,

tucking a strand of hair behind her ear. She blushed, recalling the memory of him walking through the fire, commanding the flame away from her weakened body. And then, the feel of his lips against hers, firm and full, invaded her mind.

"It's my job."

Tori had seen the devastation in his eyes before the slip into unconsciousness. Seeing her in that condition had somehow wounded him. She cleared her throat. "Thank you, Trace," she breathed. "Did everyone survive the fire? How long have I been out?" she asked in a rush. Was her father in this hospital?

"Yes, and four days." His eyes darted around the room, like he wasn't comfortable with the admission.

"Four days," she muttered. A pounding started between her ears. Eyes wide, she stared at him unblinking. She'd escaped from their family mansion in Arlington, Virginia two weeks ago with only the clothes on her back and the pendant. A week spent in one of the women's shelters where her mother had volunteered had allowed her body time to rid itself of the sedatives. Once fully alert, she'd contacted the private detective she'd hired before Denton had drugged her the first time. Looking back, it was probably that decision that had led to her incapacitation. Tori was grateful that during her absence the detective had completed his job. The detective's notes had led her to Key West. Could the struggle have been all for nothing? Her father could have been moved to another state in four days. The little money she had wouldn't get her a paper cup for water. She discovered on the trip down from Washington D.C. that cups had to be purchased at some restaurants. Why would wealthy corporations deprive their patrons of water, for goodness sake.

"No thanks necessary," he said, releasing her hand. He leaned back. After days with nothing but him in her head, the physical separation made her stomach dip into turbulent waters. The distance between them felt wrong somehow. "You want me to leave?"

Did he still have plans to walk away and not return? She needed a place to lay low while she located her father. Tori figured a guy who sat at her bedside everyday had to be one of the good ones.

"No, Trace. I want you to take me with you." He nearly fell on his ass when he jumped to his feet.

"Hold up a second," he bristled. That voice of his was burlier than she'd heard in the days past.

Tori was unfazed by his reaction. She needed help. Since he'd stayed by her side this far, he was the winner,

winner, chicken dinner by default. She reached for the tie holding her gown together behind her neck.

"Get the nurse, so we can leave." In four days, she'd be twenty-five. Four days until Denton Drake, the acting Chief Executive Officer of her family's company, would seize control of everything her father had worked his whole life to secure.

"Whoa, Beauty." Trace's voice dropped a notch. "Keep that on and let's figure a few things out."

She slipped her hands back down to her lap. "Wow, you're one of those 'what's your plan' types? What else do you want to talk about?"

He narrowed his eyes. "Your family may have something to say about you running off with a stranger."

She smiled at his veiled attempt to get information from her. It was safer if Trace didn't know she was a Currey. Plausible deniably could be his defense when Denton came for her.

"What stranger, Trace?"

"What?" he snapped. Running thick fingers through his hair.

"You heard me," she said sitting upright in the bed. "Four days you've been with me. Talking to me, helping the nurses position me. I could smell you, you know?

18

Could always tell when you left me. Your voice. Even when the darkness closed in, I'd wait to hear it in my dreams. So, I want to know how strange you think things will get between us now that I'm awake?"

"Ah..." That ink black ponytail of his, full and bushy against his neck swayed as he formulated a response.

"Very eloquent...and," she said, pointing a finger. "That's what I thought. You're trying to get rid of me."

"Don't put words in my mouth," he ground out. "Might look inappropriate if you leave the hospital with the public servant that saved you."

"Why? The good guy is supposed to get the girl," she said, her voice level. It was odd, but she trusted this stranger whose voice guided her from darkness back into light.

"I didn't say anything about me being good."

"I know. I did," she said pointing to the corner wardrobe. "Any clothes in there for me?"

"Yeah. I grabbed you a few things."

She threw the bed covers aside. "See, you are a good guy." Slowly she placed both feet on the ground. Trace was there, a broad arm around her waist, assisting her to stand. This close she could smell the clean scent of hard wood on his skin.

"Go slow," he said.

"Bossy little thing aren't you?" she teased.

He grinned, and the sharp edges of his face softened.

"Anyone mention you talk a lot?" he asked.

"To echo your words, 'among other things'," she said with a smile.

✥

Trace stared down at the woman who shocked him with her bold tongue and brazen actions. She wanted to come home with him. How the heck could he say no when she turned those eyes on him? When the medical team had arrived, she asked him to give his address to the nurse, and step out of the room. He still had no idea who she was or why she was at the fire scene. She had asked him to protect her. Now that she was awake, would she be in more danger if he left? What did he know about the events of that day? Susan, a nurse in love with Kendall's ex-husband, had started the fire. Kendall Raine was one of the female fire fighters on loan from DF&R. The emerald-eyed badass had come for a two-week assignment and fallen hard for his fellow crew member, Cutler Stevens. A former Marine, who could double for Thor, with his blond hair, blue eyes, and natural charm. Women adored him, but with Kendall in his life, the guy was so far off the market, he didn't have a product description.

Beauty emerged from the bathroom dressed in blue jeans, a Key West tie-dyed t-shirt, and flip-flops that were too big for her feet. She wiggled her toes as if getting used to the sensation of using them again. A smile came to Trace's face. Each one of her toenails was polished a different color.

"You into toes, Trace?"

Gosh, this woman was a handful. Her brown eyes sparkled with a fiery light. The intense color of the banked heat shot straight to his groin. Did she ask every question that popped into her think tank? She licked her lips and he followed the motion, hungry to repeat the movement with his own tongue. Petey Pablo's Freak-A-Leak cut through his brain. Frowning at his body's reaction to this lovely creature with the bold stare and sweet taste, he shot her a scowl.

She shrugged. "If that's your thing it's okay with me. You don't have to hide who you are."

"Beauty...enough." Pivoting on his heel, he clipped out, "Let's go."

"Fine, Beast. Grab my roses."

She laughed and walked around him, grabbing her discharge paperwork before heading for the door.

"What did you call me?" He crossed the short distance and picked up the vase with one hand.

"If I'm Beauty, then you must be the Beast," she said. "You're the big wolf man hybrid thingy."

When she opened the door, he pulled her back. "Where are you going?"

"With you." She threw up a hand. "Out the door."

"Do you know where you're going? Do you know my truck?"

She bowed at the waist and held out a hand gesturing toward the door. "After you."

"Tell me your name. I can't take you around calling you, Beauty."

"Tori," she said without hesitation.

"What were you doing at the senior citizen's village, Tori?"

He tested the name on his tongue. The four letters were too casual for her. Even with the messy hair, soot stained nails, and track marks in the bend of her elbows, she had a polished quality. Tori 'no last name' wasn't forthcoming with information.

"Trying not to die."

Siera London

He growled in frustration. Again, he thought that she had no intention of telling him more information than she had to. "Before the fire broke out."

"Oh, I was looking for someone."

Trace folded his arms over his chest. "Stop playing games. I could get burned big time for this."

She paused, and then rubbed a small hand over his forearm. "I'll tell you after we get out of here."

"Why the zero-to-sixty?"

She pulled the door open and walked into the hallway.

"I'm anxious to see my potential new boyfriend's place."

Oh no she didn't go country on him. Tori was a jokester, but he wasn't buying her routine. She was in serious trouble. When they got to his place, Trace had to figure out how to help her and keep his hands to himself. The way she touched him, a light stroke here, a soft caress there, was about to drive him crazy. And her mouth…, that sharp tongue of hers he could put to wicked use for hours. He had a difficult task ahead of him. Tori had asked him to take her home. He hoped she understood he took care of what was his, even if it was just a temporary holding. Trace would discover who had her on the run and the role

Commanding Fire

he'd have to play.

Chapter Three

Tori crossed the patio deck again. Trace's condo was built inside a nature preserve overlooking a golf course. Once they'd entered the gated community, he'd driven her down each secluded cul-de-sac, orienting her to the basics—security guard station, the pool cabana, and the clubhouse. The moment she walked through the door, a sense of freedom assailed her. The downstairs was a big box sectioned into a small kitchen when you entered, a half bath and then a quaint living area that led to a screened-in porch. A two-seater Dade County Pine swing hung from the balcony overhead. Tori instantly fell in love with the place.

"I can cook," she blurted out. She had to contribute something. After all, Trace was willingly sharing his piece of heaven with her.

"Green bananas with taro leaf?" His tall frame seemed to dwarf even the great outdoors as he stood in the open doorway.

He thought to stump her, but she just smiled. "I prefer my taro boiled with cheese on the side." She'd spent the summer following high school graduation traveling throughout the American Samoas. Her palate was well tested.

He looked surprised that she had knowledge of the Samoan people.

"You cook it. I'll eat it," Trace nodded and smiled. She got the impression his smiles were rare. She would try to give him more reasons to laugh while she was here.

Tori worked hard at learning to care for herself. Servants had been at her side since birth, but she prided herself on experiencing what the people around her did to earn their way in life. She could cook, clean, do laundry, drive, entertain like the first lady, and read the Wall Street financials with breakfast. Her father had been proud of her accomplishments. Even though his colleagues gave her the side eye, Alfred Currey lauded his only child's creative nature. Admittedly, she had an impulsive streak that often times had earned her the hairy eyeball when her mother had been alive, but her messes always worked out in the end.

"What's upstairs?" She was already headed in that direction when he responded.

"That's where we sleep."

There was that drop in his voice again.

There were no bedrooms on the first floor, so she

26

assumed they both would be sleeping on the second level. From the looks of the place, there were a total of two balconies and two porches.

"You want to show me now or later?" She waggled her eyebrows.

"Come on you little vixen."

He led them back towards the front of the house. Quickly they climbed the set of stairs along the right wall to reach a small landing. From there she could see a master bedroom to her left and a hallway bathroom. Next to it, a closet held a washer and dryer in gunmetal gray. She turned to the right and entered a smaller bedroom. The walls were painted a light, buttercup yellow to match the quilt on the bed. The room had a feminine feel to it, and instantly she knew Trace had decorated it for a young girl.

"Is this supposed to be my room?"

She glanced over her shoulder to find him watching her. Those sexy eyes were half lidded and fixed on her too big backside. Tori had a small build until you reached her hips and then everything went in-stereo. Her hips, thighs, and buttocks had a zip code of their own.

"Yeah, you can stay in here."

The words rang false. That she would be staying in his house wasn't a problem, but this room somehow felt

27

off-limits, sacred.

She raised her chin. "Take me to your room."

Trace stepped aside as if he'd been waiting for the request. Cautiously she passed him. His body heat like a summer breeze against the chill of night. Everything about the man claimed her; his scent, his voice, and his touch.

The walls in his room were painted a darker gray. A black comforter covered a massive bed with a headboard that looked like a rock climbing wall. The adjacent wall held double doors than led to a bathroom with a walk-in closet.

Trace came up behind her. He stopped shy of touching her, but she felt him. Her nipples peaked and her core tightened. He grabbed her arm and turned her around.

"Anything else you want to see?"

They stood facing each other, neither of them speaking for a moment. Where did she want to go with Trace? She'd finagled her way into his home. She knew he would keep her safe. He was a protector. Now, did she want to live out the fantasies that played in her head every time she'd heard his voice in her dreams?

"You like girls?"

A hand came down on her backside and she yelped, "Hey." The sting she expected, the tingling heat afterwards she did not. Tori's breath hitched as warmth spread across her flesh and settled in her core. Trace's eyes narrowed on her parted lips. He swore when she tilted her head up, welcoming his attentions.

"And I'll spank your ass again if you answer another one of my questions with a question."

She grimaced. "So much for Mr. Kind and Sensitive."

He wrapped an arm around her waist. "You want me to make something sensitive? Just say the word, Princess."

Tori wanted him to do just that. She wanted something unscripted with Trace. This man had stayed by her bedside, talked her back to life. He'd read to her for hours. She remembered him stroking her cheek and the brush he'd run through her hair releasing the tangles. He'd taken care of her. Even trapped inside her body, she'd sensed his loneliness. Somehow, they'd become a safe haven for each other. He could just be a decent guy looking after a girl, and she...she could be Tori for a few more days. Victoria Currey's life would catch up with her soon enough. After all, how long could a girl outrun the man with the key to her future?

Wrapping her arms as high as she could around his narrowed waist, she stepped in close, stopping when her breasts pushed against hard muscle. Lust, raw and ravenous, flared inside her. Tori mentally donned her hiking boots, necessary equipment to climb this Goliath, and bring him to his knees. Strong arms hauled her in, impossibly close. His hard length dug into her soft tummy. A gasp left her body. She looked up, their eyes locked. Her lips parted, and she breathed the word, "Princess."

❖

Princess. Trace tightened his hold around the woman in his arms. Warmth, all encompassing and smooth as slow churned butter, spread through him. How had Tori morphed an innocent word like freaking princess into the hottest two-syllables to ever hit his eardrum? She was the queen of one-word bombshells. First protect, now this shit. He was already a goner with her little body in his big mitts. The ladies cut t-shirt hugged her pert breasts, showcasing them to perfection. Over her shoulder, he trailed his eyes lower. Tori's backside was a sculpted masterpiece. Even his large hands needed a pair of hands to handle what the woman had packed in those jeans. His brain started a game of flash tag, fantasizing about all her soft curves molded beneath his hardness. Oh yeah, he could stay buried inside her for hours.

"Hey Beastie, you got money to pay for all the rides you taking with those sexy eyes of yours?"

He drew in a deep breath, not embarrassed in the least that she'd noticed him checking her out. "Not on me," he said releasing her to pat his pockets. "You take IOUs?"

Had he made a joke? The corner of her mouth lifted into a half smile like his comeback surprised her. The exchange was foreign to him, but he felt a ping in his chest. He liked that he'd put a smile on her face.

"First one's free," she laughed.

"I'm more than willing to pay my debt." Oh, what would it cost him to keep the impulsive little beauty in his home?

"If money is changing hands, you're the one who deserves the lion's share."

His eyes landed on her scarred arms. Images of the torturous acts people engaged in to support their habit tried to invade his thoughts. Giving his head a shake, he blocked them out. "You don't owe me anything." His tone firm.

She followed his gaze. Frowning, she took a step back. Aware that she'd placed distance between them, he instantly felt her cool absence on his skin.

"I'm not what you think," she snapped. "I can deal

with the stares out there." With her left hand, she pointed to the sliders leading onto his private balcony. "I hear the whispered comments...but, not from you, Trace. Not you. You understand?"

He did. When two people survived a life or death event, the shared experience forged an alliance. He'd seen her at her weakest point, the intimacy of him breathing life into her body, meant a part of him stayed with her. There would be no judgment between them because in essence, they shared a life. But, Trace said none of that. Instead, he reverted back to a general truth of his encounters with most people.

"You don't know what I'm thinking."

"Fine," she clipped. "If you want to pretend you don't see the tracks on my arms, let's get back to business. You married or got a girlfriend?"

He felt his whole body stiffen. Tori must have sensed the change in him because her face blanked of all emotion. She turned toward the door. Panic gripped him. Before she could take a step, he grabbed her arm and spun her around. "No," came his terse reply.

Her eyes lit up, a Vegas style road sign. "You want one?"

Her forwardness had surprised him in the hospital,

though he didn't let on. But this time, his mouth hung open.

Her mouth twisted in a grimace. "Too direct?" From there, the conversation took off without him. "Sorry, I caught you with a Tori *Special Edition* in the gut. Men expect women to be demure and shy. I can be, but I have to focus. It's just—"

Trace inhaled a steadying breath. The stream of words made him dizzy. "Stop."

She cast wide eyes up to him. "What did I say?"

What hadn't she said? "Where the heck did all that come from?"

"Out of my mouth," she teased. "It's a relevant question."

"To what, Beauty?"

"You brought me home, so I want to understand the nature of our arrangement."

"There's no arrangement, woman. I haven't agreed to anything."

She glanced down at the erection standing long and proud behind his zipper.

"Oh," she said pointing at his groin. "I thought you had."

Rising up on the tips of her toes, she brushed a kiss

across his lips. Softness. The first contact was that of velvet against his skin, and then the delicate cool taste of honeydew touched his tongue. Fingers, sure and eager, touched his stomach. The hem of his shirt began a slow cruise up his abdomen. His skin sizzled with her every touch as she moved higher, and then higher up his big body. As she touched him, her delicate fingertips glided, as if she were mapping him into her memory. Near his navel, she hit a rise, and then a dip, and her fingers paused. Trace cataloged everything she gave him in those brief seconds. In his mind, he filed snap shots of every burn like he could visualize his body's reaction before his eyes, every valley she touched, and then he trapped her wrist, stopping her. She looked up at him, those doe eyes marred in confusion. When she would have settled back onto her feet, he lifted her up in of his massive arms, until they were face to face. Her curves relaxed against the sculpted planes of his chest. Need fired through his veins. Hardened nipples brushed his pecs and he had to clench his fist to tamp down his instinct to claim.

"How about we take the merry-go-round tonight instead of the scream machine?" Wrong move, Trace thought as he held Tori in his arms. The pulse in his pants agreed, but he wasn't in the habit of sleeping with women on the fly. She tempted him beyond sanity, true. But when he looked into her eyes, he wanted more than one night of pleasure and there were *things* that needed to be discussed before clothes hit the floor.

She dropped a kiss on his nose. "Okay," she beamed. "I can do that."

Tori seemed confident, but Trace was already praying he could make it through the night with this vibrant woman heating up a lot more than just his life.

Chapter Four

Tori bent to smell her roses. Trace had placed them on the bar. The small marble topped island separated the kitchen from the living space. On bare feet, she moved to peer around Trace's broad back. "How much longer till dinner?"

He was at the range top where a few stalks of broccoli laid in a steamer basket. His hair hung loose down his back, a river of black satin. She grabbed two handfuls, burying her face in the heavy mass.

He laughed. "Keep distracting me and it's Mickey D's for you."

She frowned. "Can I use your phone?"

He looked over his shoulder. "Checking in with someone?" He watched her face, studying her expression.

She ducked her head, not wanting to lie to him. "Just something I need to look up."

He gestured to the ottoman beyond the bar stools. "Check there first. If no luck, check the valet in my bedroom."

When she turned to go, a hand landed on her backside.

"Don't be gone too long. I'm starving."

The desire in his voice fell over her like raw silk. His mouth twitched in a playful gesture she hadn't noticed before. The look suited him.

She grinned. "Me too." Before she could be distracted by the heated looks he bestowed her with, Tori bounded up the stairs. She needed privacy. Trace had avoided the senior village on the drive home. It was too late for visiting hours, but maybe tomorrow she could get away to see her father. She prayed he'd fared better than her under the care of Denton's private medical staff. She rubbed at the track marks on her arms. Lifting her shirt, she pulled Trace's phone from her waistband. With him in the kitchen, it had been easy to tuck it beneath her shirt. Her Internet search provided her with the senior village layout and visiting hours. Hopefully the personal bank account she'd established during her college travels abroad was still open. She punched in her password. *Invalid password* appeared in red letters. She sucked in a breath. Cut off. She exited the screen before the tears could start.

Currey Industries had total control of her life, her money, and her house until she turned twenty-five. If at that time Tori were to be married, she or her husband would assume a position equal to her father's and her trust fund would be turned over to her. If she remained unmarried, twenty-five percent of her trust would be donated to one of her mother's charities and her position in the company would be opened to a qualified applicant for a five-year term. When her father ran the company, she hadn't seen a problem with the stipulations of her trust. Her father was an honorable man that would never abandon her, but since his heart attack, the interim executive officer had assumed control of her affairs. Tori's life had changed dramatically.

"Tori." Trace's voice echoed up to the second floor. "Dinner."

"Coming," she called, wiping at her eyes. Dropping the phone on to the valet, she pasted on a smile.

Half way down the stairs, she could smell the distinct scent of coconut milk and grilled fish wafting up to greet her. Her stomach growled.

"Woman, I don't like my food cold."

She jumped down the last step. "Me neither," she replied, turning the corner. "I knew we were a perfect match."

Trace stood next to one of the dinette chairs. Two plates were on the table. Whole grilled fish, chopped potatoes, and broccoli were on one plate. The other boasted the same meal, but double the portions. She gave Trace a curious look. Could he really eat that much food in one meal?

"I'm a man, Princess," he said to her silent question.

She took note of his toned muscle. Tori wondered how soft his skin would be over all that hard-packed steel. "I can see that," she said taking a seat.

She expected one of his looks when she was too blunt, instead he laughed. He'd done that a lot in the past few hours.

"Sit. Eat."

Trace dug in without another word. Each mouthful he followed with a swig from his beer bottle. When he noticed her watching him, he stilled.

"You want one?"

She involuntarily recoiled. After what she'd suffered, the drugs, the hellish days and nights without control of her own body, she didn't think she could ever imbibe. "No...no, thank you."

Trace narrowed his eyes. She dropped her head and ate in silence. God, he probably thought she was a whack-job.

"Tori, look at me." When she dragged her gaze to his, he winked. "I get it."

She appreciated that he didn't force more answers than she was willing to give. Not yet. Trace made her feel comfortable. She wanted to tell him everything, but then...she'd made that mistake before. The need to give him some truth about her life tugged at her heart.

"I used to drink...before this."

He looked at her arms. Unlike most people who quickly looked away, his eyes took on a faraway look. Who in his life had arms that looked like hers she wondered.

✜

Trace put the last of the dishes in the automatic washer. He'd given Tori the job of arranging the leftovers packed in storage containers in the refrigerator. He felt her presence behind him.

He turned to find her in his personal space. That sweet melon scent he'd first noticed in the hospital poured off her now.

"I need a spoon," she said. Her voice came out too soft, and where he had been semi-hard since she'd buried her hands in his hair, he could hammer nails now.

"What for?" With his stomach full, his libido was

hungry for another type of feast.

She grinned and lifted a half-gallon of chocolate mint ice cream to his mouth.

He shook his head. "You're going to be wired if you eat that."

She blew him an air kiss. And dang, he wanted to catch the thing and put it in his pocket.

"I'm always wired."

He fished in the tray of clean utensils in the stainless-steel basket beside the sink. Pulling free a spoon, he handed it to her. "Anything else you need, Princess?"

The clink of the washer signaling the timer had been set seemed to be an on button for Tori.

Removing the lid, she pushed the spoon deep into the soft center. Damn, Trace nearly creamed in his boxers. Did she have any idea how sexy she was? The way she danced from one idea to the next without pretense, he suspected she had no inkling of the power she held over anything with a Y chromosome.

"Open up, Beastie."

He hesitated for a second. She raised a brow, giving him a mock grimace. Bending, he opened his mouth for her. When she slid the spoon between his lips, her own lips parted. The icy sweetness against the warmth of his mouth felt incredible. Shit, what was she doing to him? He'd eaten everything he'd cooked tonight a hundred times and yet, in her presence, every spice was amplified. He must have made a sound.

"Good?"

He looked at her. "The best I've ever had," he said.

She licked her lips and this time, he did use his tongue to taste her. Real slow, his licked and nibbled on her lower lip, before sucking the fullness in his mouth. The need to possess her, claim her, overwhelmed him, but he'd promised himself he'd go slow with her. Let her grow to trust him with her secrets. So far, she hadn't divulged anything about her past. He noticed she could boost a phone, but he didn't call her on it.

"Take me to bed, Trace," she whispered.

"I will," he hesitated, "when you show me who you really are."

He walked past her and out of the kitchen. It was the hardest thing he'd ever done. Not just because he had a stiff one wedged against his thigh, either.

❖

Tori plopped down on the cowhide couch next to

Trace. He didn't scoot away when their arms touched, so she stayed put. How many days did she have before Denton found her? If she only had hours, she'd give every second to the man beside her.

"So," she said, looking up into his dark eyes, framed by custom lashes. That was the only way a man could be blessed with thick and lush everything. "We've established that you prefer the opposite sex." He shot her a scowl before snatching the TV remote off the table and flicking the on switch.

"If you want me to spank your ass, just ask, Tori. You don't have to piss me off."

"Hum, I'll keep that in mind." She swung around, feet resting on the couch and dropped her head into his lap.

He glanced down at her and turned off the television. "You want to play?"

"Maybe. But first, I have another question."

"If it's a question you know the answer to, then be prepared to roll over. Ass up."

"Okay. You're definitely an ass man." He growled and moved to get off the couch. "No, I meant into the female ass. You like my ass."

He grunted.

When he didn't say anything, she sandwiched his lips

between her thumb and forefinger. "Oh, come on. Throw a girl a compliment. I'm insecure about my body."

He erupted in laughter. "Liar. That's why you basically stripped at the hospital?"

"Oh, that," she chided. "That was therapeutic."

"For who?"

"Us. Compatibility is important, Trace, even with roommates."

"So now we are roommates? You gonna sleep in your bed tonight."

"Not if I can help it."

She hated sleeping alone. Denton had hired private duty nurses to *care* for her. The drugs kept her in a near comatose state, locked in a bed, alone, always alone in the quiet.

"Ask your question, Tori."

"You read romance novels to me."

He shifted beneath her, his fingers stroking her scalp.

"Yeah."

"Were they your books?"

He stopped moving. Not even his abdomen shifted with the inhale.

"They belonged to my best friend."

"A woman?" Why had he kept them? She'd seen

45

every inch of his home. No woman had been in this home in a long time, or maybe never.

"That's right."

"You're keeping them for her?"

"Tori," he ground out. "I told you I was unattached."

"Except you're attached to another woman's romance novels."

He released a frustrated sigh. "She liked them. I thought you might, too."

"You read to her while she was in the hospital, too."

He tried to get up then, but she rolled onto her side, snaking both arms around his waist. The action brought her cheek in contact with the erection they both had tried to ignore.

"I used to."

There was something about his answer that sounded final.

"This woman...she hurt you?"

"No. She died."

Tori sucked in a breath at the anger in his tone. It was obvious the death still affected him. Knowing that someone had damaged him in any way angered her. Trace was kind, thoughtful, and generous in a hulky 'you need a spanking' way. His muscles bunched beneath her fingers and she thought to change the subject.

"You were right about the stories. I like them, except..."

"Except," he quizzed, the hand in her hair tightening on the strands.

"We didn't finish Gideon and Lina's story. How does he convince her to stay with him?"

"The book is in the car. I'll put it in your room."

"No, I want you to read it to me, like before."

Their eyes met and held. "Why is that?"

"The sound of your voice, I...I like..."

The hand he'd threaded through her strands, gave a slight tug on the roots. "The rest," he said.

"I like the way you take care of me," she whispered.

"Tori."

"Yes?"

"No more talking," he said, covering her mouth with his.

Her plan was to allow him a sample, whetting his appetite for more to come. Trace wanted nothing to do with appetizers. He pushed his tongue into her mouth, feasting. Tori came on board, fast. His command of their kiss was soft and hard. A tender stroke followed by a demanding bite. She didn't know what to expect. She

47

loved it. Now, if she could just get Trace to unleash the passion she knew he held back.

Chapter Five

Trace didn't want to take advantage this woman. So, why was he flirting with Tori, kissing her? Freaking romance books. She lay curled in his lap like a contented kitten until he read the last page.

She kicked at the couch's armrest. "Why aren't the other couple married?" she raged after he finished reading the epilogue.

"They have a second book in the series."

"Oh," she smiled. "What are you waiting for? Let's get some popcorn for book two."

Trace was hard as a rock with Tori's mouth so close to his junk.

"No, I've reached my limit." More like he teetered on the edge of his control. The urge to take her, push inside her body and stay there was a repetitive command in his head, and a warrior followed orders. He needed to get her out of the house. It was after seven. Happy Hour at Hobo Alley would be in full swing if they left now. His community was on the other side of the Cow Key Bridge, so it took him about fifteen minutes to get to downtown Key West and another five to reach their destination. The fire fighters had a designated table at the bar and grill located on the west end of Old Town Key West. Tori could meet his firehouse crew. Conversation came easy to Tori, so she'd fit right in. He tucked a stray curl behind her ear. "How about I take you out tonight, Princess?"

Shaky, the part-time bouncer greeted them at the swing doors. The place was the ultimate man cave with dark plank floors, wooden tables, and non-stop beer. It sat on the corner of Eaton and Key West's infamous Duval Street. Attractions, like the President's Summer White House and Ernest Hemmingway's home were blocks away. Twin windows the size of double doors faced east to the Atlantic Ocean and west toward the Gulf of Mexico. In addition to the prime real estate, there was a room-length bar and a live band that started up at ten o'clock.

"Trace," he stared at Tori. "When did you get a girl?"

Shaky followed them inside like Trace had suddenly become more interesting. And maybe he had. Since he'd joined the firehouse crew, Trace had avoided serious relationships. No meeting friends, no dates, and definitely no sleepovers. For six years and counting that had been his reality until today.

"Shaky. Don't follow me. She's real."

The owner, Rachel Hoberstein, was behind the counter when he walked through the door with Tori on his heels. She too stared at him with her mouth hanging open.

Nathan Zachary, the arson investigator on staff sat with his wife, Symphony, nestled between his powerful long legs. Her pregnant belly was visible from the door. Symphony had been hired as a waitress while Nathan had been on assignment at DF&R Station 58. With her midnight, blue tresses and amber eyes, Nate had been a goner the first time he laid eyes on the butterscotch beauty. When her name made the suspect list in one of Nathan's arson cases, him signing the arrest warrant had nearly destroyed them both. Trace still wasn't sure how Nathan had won her back.

"What's up, Trace?" Adam asked, his voice falling faint when he noticed his plus one. Adam, Symphony's former neighbor and honorary godfather, occupied the seat next to them. A long neck beer bottle suspended at his lips.

Cutler and Kendall had their heads together at the same highboy table. When they looked up and saw him, Cutler waved him over. His friends smiled and called out familiar greetings, until they noticed the petite woman at his back. Nathan looked down right puzzled while Symphony had a loony smile on her face. Cutler came to his feet, while Kendall studied Tori like an interrogator ready to pull out the cuffs.

Tori tightened her hand on his fingers. Trace smiled. So, she wasn't totally fearless. He didn't know why that pleased him. It was nice to know that she leaned on him for strength.

"What's up?" Trace asked when he approached the hot guys table. The verbiage wasn't his. Claudia, the head waitress at Hobo's called the table that and it had stuck.

Nathan was the first to speak. "You're the girl from the senior village fire."

Nathan's piercing gray eyes seemed to dissect Tori. She moved to step away from him, but Trace pulled her back. He gave him a curious glance over her shoulder.

"Hi. It's nice to meet more of Trace's friends."

His crew was cool, but he'd never brought a woman into the circle before. He didn't know how long Tori would be around, but he didn't want her drilled with questions. At least, not before he could do the asking.

Kendall frowned. "We are Trace's only friends," she said, a hint of defensiveness in her tone.

"Not anymore," she chirped. "He has me."

Trace shook his head, but inside, he wore a big, stupid grin. She was staking her claim on him within the group. Was her motivation to get the five pairs of eyes off her arms? It was just like Tori to give anyone that thought to intimidate her a giant *bird*. That middle finger of hers sprouting a verbal wingspan with enough power to circle the bar twice over. They all needed to back off Tori, especially Kendall. Before joining their crew, Kendall had been married to the Chief of Police in Cockrell, Texas. The physical abuse she'd suffered at his hand made her naturally suspicious of new people, and fiercely protective of those she held dear. Trace was proud to be counted amongst her friends, but he wouldn't tolerate an aggression aimed at his princess. Cutler, sensing the change in his mood, placed a hand on his fiancée's neck, caressing.

"Tori this everybody. Everybody this is Tori. Done with introductions," Trace said, pulling her to the other end of the table.

Without thinking, he grabbed her around the waist, and placed her on a stool. The proverbial music stopped. Shoot. All eyes were on them.

Cutler smiled and tipped his bottle in their direction. "Welcome, Tori. I'm Cutler Stevens. This sexy redhead is my soon-to-be ball and chain, Kendall. This here," he continued pointing to Nathan, "fella with the dark glossy hair is Nathan Zachary, with his little momma, Symphony. Adam is the crusty barnacle who completes the group."

Trace had taken up a position behind Tori's seat, scowling at all his friends. He could feel Tori's smile.

"Hi all. It's great to meet you."

Kendall asked, "Got a last name, Tori?"

Trace moved closer, pressing his front against Tori's back. Tori squirmed in her seat, stopping only when her back pressed into his erection. He grunted, but didn't put more space between them.

She reached up over her shoulder and stroked his chest.

"Sorry," she whispered.

He grunted in reply.

"What?" he growled, at the table. "Drink your damn beers."

Symphony waved one of the white cocktail napkins. "Since when do you use profanity?"

"Since my friends started staring like I have a third eye."

That seemed to reset everyone's clock. The attention went from Tori to him, but he feared the damage had already been done. Her rigid posture called to his protective instinct. Those scars on her arms broadcast a story before she ever opened her mouth. It pissed him off that the Twitter version of her life was trending with his

54

friends. Instinctively, he slid a protective arm around her waist. This time, those lovely curves of hers met his like oil and water. No, there was no melting into his body. And didn't that piss him off all the more.

"Claudia," he called out, needing a beer in the worst way.

Adam gave a smirk. "She's supposedly out sick, but I heard talk of her new cowboy keeping her busy, if you catch my meaning."

Cutler chuckled. "Roy Orbison could catch that 'TMI' hard pitch."

"Rachel is swamped," Adam continued. "We're all nursing the first beer. Gotta make this puppy last."

Conversation had returned to normal, but not for him. Tori shifted on her stool in front of him. The witty banter they shared in the quiet of his home had dried up. He pressed his lips to her temple. When she angled her head, increasing the contact, he nestled his back around hers. His wide body swallowed her up, but she relaxed and sank into his arms. Perfection, he thought. "You okay now, Princess?" he whispered in her ear.

"Better now," she mouthed. The succulent scents of melon and mint tingled in his nose. He breathed her in, his body already addicted to her scent, and just like that, he was ready for some below the waist action.

"Oh, I just thought of something." Her spine straightened abruptly, forcing him to take a step back.

"What's that?" Before she answered him, she circled his wrist with those small hands. Trace noticed how soft Tori was compared to him. No rough spots on her body, rather the only sharp edges stemmed from her personality. What kind of life had she led before coming to him? A polished woman capable of a lethal bite.

"I can wait tables."

"No," Trace said. He wanted to keep her close to him, but she had already hopped down off her perch.

"Come on. I won't disappear on you."

Damn. She was right. He was afraid he would look up and she'd have vanished on him. He gotten used to spending his days with her.

Trace took Tori over to the bar and introduced her to Rachel. When Tori mentioned that she had bar experience, Rachel welcomed the help. Within a couple of hours Tori had the bar running like an assembly line.

Trace relaxed and watched her work.

"Hey, man. What's the story?" Cutler had moved to his end of the table.

"No story," Trace said, placing his empty bottle on

the tabletop.

"Is that why you can't take your eyes off her? She's a victim. You pulled her from the fire."

Fury erupted in Trace's blood. He turned on his friend, a growl bursting from his throat. "She needed a place to stay." That got everybody's attention.

"She's staying with you?" A furrow pulled Kendall's brows low. "Who is she? Where did she come from?"

Symphony, with a hand over her seven-month belly said, "Trace, we're just worried about you. You've been spending a lot of time with her."

Trace felt the need to defend himself. "I pulled her from that fire. She's my responsibility."

A few pair of bugged eyes regarded him. Nathan spoke in a low tone. "Look, we all feel a certain connection to the people we help, but bringing her into your home—,"

Trace didn't need a lecture. "Look, your permission isn't required. Mind your business. Tori just needs time to—,"

Cheers erupted around the bar. Some tourists had wandered in, but several of the locals had their beers raised in song. At first all he saw was hair. Tori's walnut tresses twirled around as she tossed her head to and fro. Trace realized that if he could see her above the crowd, she stood on something very tall...like the bar counter. He cursed. Tori's voice carried over the jukebox, but it was the gyrations she repeated for the roaring crowd that painted his vision red. Abruptly, he shot off his stool, the thing tilted before hitting the floor.

"Oh, man," Cutler's voice, pitched higher than normal. "She does a good wrecking ball."

There were a few gasps. Adam cleared his throat.

"What are you talking–" Symphony's voice was drowned out by Nathan's. "She's a spitfire."

Miley Cyrus's song droned on in the background with Tori singing like she owned a golden gramophone mounted on a wooden base. She was oblivious to the human wrecking ball demolishing everything in his path to reach her. The sight of her licking a beer bottle sent the crowd into a frenzy and him into a rage. A drunk patron was reaching for her leg, when Trace gripped her around the knees and tossed her over his shoulder.

She gasped at the impact. "Ah—,"

He cut her off. "Don't say a word," he growled. "I'm taking you home."

Kendall called to him above the booing crowd. "Go easy on her, Trace."

Not likely to happen.

Chapter Six

Tori panted to catch her breath. Trace placed her in the front seat of his GMC Sierra and slammed the door. His eyes had darkened. The stare he aimed at her penetrated her depths with laser precision. Moving away from the scorching cut wasn't an option in the small space. Why was he scowling? She tucked her lip between her teeth and waited.

When he climbed inside and stabbed the key into the ignition, she realized all the elation she felt was not a shared experience. Trace was furious, but he wasn't talking. Well, she would remove that option from the table.

"That was fun," she giggled. When he hit her with a fierce growl, she pressed one hand over her mouth, stifling her laughter. Recognizing he was not happy with her, Tori cranked her enthusiasm down a notch. "What? Too much, again?"

Trace gripped the steering wheel. The skin over his knuckles stretched thin and pale, like the moonlight through the windshield. A flash of unease skirted through her. Was he refusing to talk with her?

"Stop brooding and use your words," she balked.

He turned away from the road. "You want me to do something for you?"

It was after midnight. A1A headed north was deserted this time of night. All the partygoers were behind them on Duval Street. She recalled the undergraduate Duval Crawl with her sorority sisters from Johns Hopkins University. Maybe, she would add a pub run to her list.

"Yes," she said, satisfied he'd gotten the signal to lighten up.

"Let's do an even exchange. You don't shake your ass for other men." He kept his eyes on the road, but she still felt the weight of his stare from earlier.

Her breath hitched. Was he jealous? She had to know. "Are you seeing green because of what I did for the Hobos?"

He cut her a sideways glance. "You're pushing your luck."

"Trace, I need your support. Don't be upset."

"Not with the bar act. Too late. You're never going there again." It was the fastest rush of words she'd received to date. Seeing this tough guy struggle to reign in his anger sobered her. Replaying his dictate got her attention.

"You can't do that. I need a job."

"It's done."

"You're not the boss of me," she railed.

Trace had the gall to smile. "Let's test your theory," he snapped.

Anger caught fire in her belly. "You want an exchange. How about you tell your friends it's rude to stare. To punish by association," she yelled. Why had she let complete strangers make her feel dirty, a human stain? The compulsion to go on the attack had sizzled through her veins, charging every nerve ending with an electric current. As Trace's tribe of friends assessed her rightness for him she saw two things reflected in their eyes—pity or predator. Either way, she came up lacking. Waiting the tables had helped to rebalance her mental scales, control the impulses. But then, she'd glanced over and saw Cutler questioning Trace. The strain was evident around his mouth as he spoke. He was being judged and found guilty by association. The leash on her control had snapped.

The truck slowed its forward motion before coming to a complete halt. The red light didn't stop the movie reel in her head. She'd done the right thing by getting them out of there.

"Tori..." His voice was too gentle. "You did that, on

the bar, for me?"

The awe in his voice tugged at her heartstrings. Concentrate, she told herself, as emotion threatened to overwhelm her. Out of the corner of her eye, she regarded him. "For me, too."

He pressed his lips together. Narrowed brown eyes softened in comprehension. "Those impulses you mentioned earlier," he waited a beat, "needed an outlet?"

She drew a nervous hand across her temple. "Yes, something like that." His expression blanked. And she didn't know if she should be happy or sad. On one hand, there was no judgment. On the other, the connection she'd felt whenever he was near, dimmed.

The traffic light flashed green. They were in motion again. Trace signaled, turned left and drove them down Atlantic Ocean Boulevard. He put the car in park and cut the engine when they reached Higgs Beach. The tropical scents of royal palm, butterfly orchids, and aloe from the West Martello Fort, now home to the local garden club, seeped in through the sunroof.

Trace let out a sigh, deep and tremulous. Regret welled inside her for causing him distress.

"I can take care of us, Tori. Only one of us has a rescue badge and you don't have to work."

Did he realize what he was saying? He didn't know a thing about her, not even her last name. It cut deep that she couldn't be totally honest with him, but she wanted their time together to be special. Wanted him to remember she was the woman that protected him as fiercely as he did her.

"I know you can, but..." Already, her being with him had changed his life. Not for the better, either.

"But?"

"You shouldn't have to. Your friends don't like that you're with me."

He took her hand in his. "I agreed to your coming home with me. I knew what that entailed."

"Well, I want to take care of myself." After six months under lock and key, Tori needed this taste of freedom. These few days would have to carry her through a lifetime of pain and regret.

"That's all it is?"

A golf cart holding two women pulled along side them. They giggled as one bet the other who could reach the warm water first. Both climbed from the front bench, stumbling toward the water in the darkness. Nothing impeded their steps.

"What else would it be?" she asked watching them

65

wade into the ocean. As she watched the pair twist and turn in slow motion, she thought on the luxury of time. It was a commodity she could ill afford.

"Maybe, you're trying not to tie yourself to me. Not leave any debts behind."

She averted her gaze, not wanting Trace to see his truth reflected in her eyes. Strong fingers gripped her chin.

"Don't look away, Princess."

Tori couldn't deny him. She glanced up and over. Tears stung her eyes. "Trace," her voice shook. "Don't ask."

In her heart, she knew he wouldn't listen.

"How long can you stay, Tori?"

Loaded question. When she'd first met Denton at her father's offices, he'd been a needed friend. At seventeen, she'd just lost her mother to an aneurysm and she'd been flattered that a young man in the company was bold enough to befriend the boss's daughter. He'd encouraged her, comforted her, and said he loved her. Her hopes of marriage and a family were encouraged by his attentions. Denton's aspirations stopped and started with his career, but that didn't matter.

"Princess?" She heard Trace say.

Princess, indeed. Tori had enough whimsical dreams

for the both of them. Blinded by her own naivety, she'd missed the signs of Denton's future treachery. She and her father had grown to trust him. Truly, he was an extension of their family. He was always at the Currey estate, attending society functions on her arm; he had been a steadying force at a time when chaos ruled her life. Less than a year after her mother's death, when her father had suffered his second heart attack, he'd asked Denton to look after his affairs...including Tori. The school of business at Johns Hopkins had been Denton's idea. Tori learned to control her impulses after he arranged for private therapy and she thrived in her curriculum. She'd hoped their personal relationship would flourish. They could manage Currey Industries together, but things had begun to change between them. Denton no longer made suggestions, but instead he issued orders. The Currey *name* was all he needed to garner obedience.

Denton had control of everything, and everyone around him. She and her father were expendables. In hindsight, she and her father had helped him to imprison them. She closed her eyes, shutting out reality. The truth was, even sitting in this truck, she was still on the run. Borrowed time was all she and Trace had. Being with Trace had inextricably changed her at an elemental level.

Now, all she dreamed of was more time with him.

Though she didn't want to, she opened her eyes because she didn't want to miss a second of seeing his handsome face. "I don't know," she whispered.

He nodded. She was sure he told himself he understood her reasons. Was he now questioning her motivations for coming home with him? Did he regret pulling her from that fire, and thus into his life?

"Let me help you. Tell me who you are. Who's after you?"

She shook her head, vigorously rejecting his suggestion. "You can't stop him."

His eyes narrowed and his fingers clenched tight on her chin. "You mean you don't trust me to protect you," he growled.

She jerked as if he had slapped her. "I trust you. I want to spend what time I have with you."

"So, you're using me?"

She tilted her head, so she could see his eyes clearly.

"No," she said brushing a hand across his cheek. He'd done the same to her a dozen times.

Before she knew what was happening, Trace leaned across the cab, undid her seat belt and pulled her into his lap.

"Explain," he growled.

She looked up into his face. His eyes seemed to sparkle in the moonlight streaming through the windshield. A rich spice clung to him. She moved closer, their noses touching, and inhaled him.

"I want you to use me," she said. "As much as you want, Trace. I want to give you whatever you need." He'd stayed with her simply because she'd asked. She knew he wouldn't take anything from her, but she hoped he'd accept what she offered freely.

He made a throaty sound of frustration. "Except who you really are."

The way he stared at her made her heart ache. The look was protective, yet condemning.

"Please, Trace. Don't reject me." She probably sounded needy, but she didn't care when it came to Trace. She'd beg him not to send her away. Plead with him to touch her. This close she could see the angles of his face sharpen.

"For the record, our scars are a part of who we are, not the whole. No explanation required. Not to me, not to my friends. And, I'm not going to be okay if I come home and you're not there."

With that, Trace buried his hands in her dark curls,

Commanding Fire

and covered her lips with his mouth. They both groaned at the contact. Lust flared to life inside her. When he worked his hands down her torso, she shifted until he held her round ass in both hands. Wiggling around the steering wheel she got her knees on either side of his hips. Her panties were drenched and she ached all over for his touch. Sensing her need, Trace adjusted her position until her heated sex cradled his erection through his jeans. He broke their kiss and she whimpered.

"As much as I want starts now."

Oh, he was definitely the boss of her.

Chapter Seven

Trace should have been ticketed for all the laws he broke getting them back home. Though Tori had no problem surrendering to him with a steering wheel pressed into her back, there was no way he'd treat her like a one-night stand. He wanted their first time together to be in his bed. When they'd entered the townhouse, the enticing aroma of roses permeated the air. All of a sudden, he was glad she'd insisted on bringing her flowers home. They reminded him of her. That she had chosen to stay with him.

The door to the master bathroom opened, light joined by shadow cut a path into the dimly lit bedroom, popping Trace to the here and now. He sat up, his eyes locked on the elegant vision before him. A wall of steam surrounded Tori, but that's not what held his attention. She was gloriously bare. Full breasts with pert nipples, damp and beaded, sat high on her chest. Her waist was that of a woman capable of handling a man his size. And then there were her hips, round and shapely, and he could already feel the tingle in his palms, the anticipation of possessing her. He imagined how beautiful she'd be rounded with his child. He wanted a little girl with Tori's zest for life and generous nature. As he continued to enjoy the view, Tori cocked her head to the side.

"Why aren't you naked?" Trace glanced down. He'd toed off his boots and shoes, shucked his cargo pants. All that remained was his t-shirt and boxers. "Don't tell me you don't put out on the first night?" she teased.

And didn't that pull his head back into the game. He jackknifed off the mattress, stalking toward her. Tori, being Tori, didn't stand by like an innocent waiting to be taken. No, she rushed forward, reaching for him with her arms outstretched.

"You are the most beautiful woman in the world," he breathed. He'd always thought it sounded silly when men said lines like that to women. Now he totally got it. He could spew sappy words to Tori forever and they would never be lies. She was gorgeous, and he was proud to make her his.

The moment they touched, his shaft grew another inch. His heart pumped a steady rhythm, despite the tremor he felt in his hand when he cupped her nape in one hand and her sex in the other. She stroked a hand over his cheek, and he turned fully into her palm. The electricity, when it zipped through his veins, charged him to full capacity. When he looked down, her eyes were at half mast, her lips parted. On a groan, he lowered his head and pressed his lips to hers. Her tongue met his. Sparks flashed all around them, cocooning them in. The only thing for them to touch...was each other. All his brain registered was soft, warm, and mine. Trace pulled her closer, his fingers moving over her cleft.

"Mine," he whispered, as their kiss ended. Breaths sawing in and out of their lungs.

Her folds were slick and emotion swelled in his chest that she was more than ready for him. Gently, he parted her there, and oh, her scent filled his nose, and his mouth watered. He imagined her honey flowing over his tongue, feeding him, slaking his hunger.

"You started without me, Princess?"

Up on her tiptoes, she nipped at his lower lip. The sting cut straight through his control and he tightened his hold.

"I wanted to make sure you rounded first, second, and third bases," she said. "Let me help you."

Trace stiffened when she gathered his shirt in her hands, tugging the material higher. She was too short to tear the material over his head, so he bent forward helping her. When he came to his full height, light streaming from the door behind them, illuminated his skin. He watched as Tori's eyes blazed a heated trail from his abdomen up his sternum. He heard her breath hitch, and then she gasped. She'd seen his scar. Eight inches of dark memories and failure carved into the area between his sternum and navel. Shame threatened to crush him. Oh...she was touching the raised flesh. First, with the pads of her fingers, and then with her palm. When moist heat caressed his skin, he nearly shot his load. His scar didn't repulse her.

"You've been hiding." He tensed, ready for her to reject him. "This hot body from me, Beastie. Maybe, you should ride the bench as punishment."

His heart and his head blew their lids. He laughed, overwhelmed by her care, her compassion, and her acceptance of him. He enfolded her in his arms. She smelled like the first rain on a summer night, fresh and heated, rich in heady sweetness. "I'm about to knock the ball out of the park, Princess."

"I hope so because I'm about to give you a fast pitch," she crooned.

With her lips, she blazed a trail of heated kisses in and around his pecs, sucking the turgid peaks into the heat of her mouth. She continued to play and he allowed it, reveled in it. He grit his teeth against the assault of sensations coursing through his body, commanding him to take her now, hard and fast. Then she changed direction. Her kisses traveled down his sternum to his abdomen. He hissed when her warm breath blew across his length.

"Tori," he breathed.

She looped her thumbs in the waist of his boxers and tugged the soft cotton south. His length sprang free bobbing its head in expectation.

"Trace," she replied moving towards the floor. He released her nape, instead gripping her upper arm.

"What are you doing?"

Her laugh was coy and sensual when it reached his ears. A light touch on his calf, had him lifting his feet, one followed by the other, stepping out of his boxers.

Tori rose to her full height. "I thought it would be obvious," she said, gripping his sex in one hand. "What about now. Any more questions?"

"Yeah." He pushed one finger inside her. Hot. She was tight, and her slick walls clamped down on his finger pulling him deep inside. She moaned. "You on anything?" He wanted to protect her, but he didn't want any physical barriers between them tonight.

"Yes."

"I want to take you bare. You can trust me. I would

75

never put you at risk." Trace's heart beat an erratic rhythm. Would she agree? He'd never asked to ride a woman bareback before. If she planned to leave him soon, then he wanted to feel every inch of her, heart to heart, skin-to-skin, inside and out.

Her heated gaze swept over him. He recognized the twinkle in her eye, right before the smile he loved spread across her face. She wanted him with the same crazy intensity he felt.

"I want to feel you that way, too," she rasped.

He didn't need a hand-written invitation. He swept her off her feet.

"Hold your balance," he said.

"Come again?"

In the time it took her to question him. Trace had both her legs over his shoulders, her nub at his mouth. He sucked and licked at the pleasure center, locking onto her thighs when she bucked against his mouth. Her flavor burst over his tongue. Gosh, he was practically drunk on her after one taste. Her sweet moans of ecstasy reached his ears, and Trace hardened to the point of pain. He was satisfying his woman. The knowledge brought an infusion of pride like he'd never felt. This woman was his and his alone. When she began to tremble in his arms, he increased his efforts. Pushing his tongue deeper into her tender flesh, he snaked deep, until he felt the telltale spasms of impending release. Her fingers threaded into his hair and her nails scraped against his scalp. He loved that she marked him.

"Trace," she panted.

She was close. Abruptly he withdrew from her heated core and latched onto her clit. He felt her tremble. Her thighs gripped the sides of his head, and then she screamed. His name fell from her lips, over and over again.

Before the night was over, he planned to show her where she belonged. His home was hers. His bed was where she would lay her head every night. Her silken tresses would fall over his chest as he drove into her well into the late-night hours. He'd leave her dizzy with pleasure.

✜

Tori burned inside. Trace's tongue, that wicked, wicked tongue lit her up like a long, sensual torch stroking through her folds, over her clitoris. He'd called her beautiful. Everything he said and did brought her endless pleasure. He breached her core with his tongue and she grabbed ahold of his hair, pulling the strands free of the single confine. She gyrated against his mouth, driving him deeper into her body, quenching his sexual thirst with her feminine honey. Tori jerked against his mouth, but he palmed her backside in both his massive hands. The full-frontal assault continued. She breathed deep, spreading her legs wider, granting him full access to the heart of her. The tremors started slow. Each pull dragged her orgasm closer to the surface. His warm woodsy scent, the silk of his hair, the feel of his skin, it all seduced her until she let go. The pleasure when it hit, shattered her. When she thought to catch her breath, Trace had other ideas.

"I'm going to lower you. Lock your ankles around my hips." All his smooth muscles carried her as if she weighed nothing. Powerful legs strode with purpose as he took them to the bed. He didn't release her, and she wouldn't have let him go if her life depended on it. With her straddling him, he reclined against the headboard. His wide shoulders at home in this position. His manhood pulsed at her entrance and she whimpered with need.

"Trace, please."

She didn't have to wait. Dropping his head, he flicked out his tongue circling her nipple. Her back bowed, pushing her taut peak into his open mouth. A strangled cry tore from her lips as his hot steel glided up and down through her drenched sex, commanding her to give more. And she obeyed. Each passage through her nether lips coated him in her essence. Shifting, she offered her other breast. He chuckled, and rewarded her with another warm stroke of his wide tongue. Gosh, he smelled so good. His woodsy scent flared, and she inhaled, pulling every piece of him under her skin. Using his shoulders as leverage, Tori angled her hips, granting him better access to her center. The power in his body thrilled her.

"Ready, Princess?"

She stared up into his eyes. The pupils flickered like open flame. Her heart skipped a beat, the anticipation of feeling his fire, momentarily stole her breath. "Yes."

"Relax...for me, Tori. We'll go slow."

She regarded his face. A mask of barely chained lust replaced the calm she had come to expect from him.

"I don't want slow." She wanted to experience lovemaking in all its forms, raw and fast, gentle and slow, deep and ravenous, insatiable and satiated. One shift of his lower body, and Trace drove up into her hungry channel. Her sex unused to the sizable intrusion constricted, preventing his entry. Tori ordered her body to surrender.

She trusted Trace completely. Knew deep in her heart, he'd satisfied the one desire that no other man could. Instinctively, she recognized no one else would measure up to him.

"Don't worry, Princess. You'll be counting stars soon enough."

Tori inhaled a breath, willing her muscles to relax. She wanted to please Trace. Wanted him to feel how she felt about him, though she'd never admit it aloud.

"Want to touch the stars," she panted.

He adjusted her atop of him, spread her thighs wide, opening her sex like a flower. The cool air surrounding her body tingled against her swollen heat. Trace began to move. With every rotation of his hips, he opened her to him. She struggled to accept all he offered, but then he plunged deep. She cried out. His engorged flesh coaxed her resistant body into surrender, sharpening her pleasure.

He stunned her by pulling out. He threaded his fingers into her damp tresses. "I'd give the stars to you. Want you happy," he rasped before driving back into her.

"Yes...yes," she moaned, lost in him. Trace pumped into her. Each thrust spreading her wider, leaving no dark places untouched by his magic.

Trace began to ride her hard. Each stroke pushed her

through into another world, their world. Here, only sensation existed, and she clung to it. Her heels digging into his broad back, locking her to him as his muscles bunched and released beneath her hands. Smooth masculine hardness quaked beneath her fingertips.

"Tori," he said, his voice guttural and animalistic. And the leash, she thought he'd never let go of, broke. Full, penetrating strokes, delivered, again and again. Her hold on him, on her very breath, slipped and then...her body seized and exploded. Pleasure, pure as the fallen snow stripped away all pretense and she screamed his name until her throated burned hot.

Trace didn't stop. No, he pumped into her faster, his grip tightening on her backside, his heavy breathing almost tangible in the air. Sweat clung to his body. A slapping sound echoed through the room where they joined. And then his big body jerked, and he growled deep in his throat.

"Mine," and then, teeth sank into her shoulder. She screamed again as another orgasm tore through her body. Fragmenting her farther.

That one word reassembled her life with him at the center. Warmth spread through her core, milking his seed into her body, tying them together. Two bodies, one breath, and now one heart.

"Want you to stay forever," he whispered.

At his words, Tori's heart soared. Blood rushed in her veins, his desire for her, flipping and turning her upside down on love's rollercoaster, and then everything came to a screeching halt. She wanted forever too, but real life was gaining on her. Unfortunately, she'd tripped up and fallen in love...with the right man, at the wrong time.

Chapter Eight

Trace snuggled up behind Tori. Her full bottom cradled his semi-hardness, the man in the moon lounging without a care. It was Saturday morning, the crack of golf balls struck with an open club face filtered across the balcony and into his bedroom.

"You awake?" he asked pulling her closer to his body.

"I could be." He heard the laughter in her voice.

"Turn over."

She giggled and did as he asked. "I thought we tried this position already." They were face-to-face now.

"Woman, get your mind out of my boxers."

"Oh, I thought I had gotten rid of all of those last night."

"We can arrange that," he laughed.

"Please do."

She trailed her fingers down his abdomen.

"You ready to talk about the room across the hall and this scar?"

He wasn't, but for her he'd try. After their second lovemaking session, she'd asked him about the wound.

Instead, he'd pulled her beneath him and loved her past the point of exhaustion.

"It was my sister's room."

"Oh." Trace could hear the surprise in Tori's voice.

"So," her voice soft, "the best friend and the books...belonged to your sister."

When he didn't say anything more, she tried to circle his body and pull him in for an embrace. It had been a long time since another comforted him. That it was her, pleased him. It felt good to mention his sister. Time had faded the bad memories under the bright light of the good times they had shared.

"After she finished college, the plan was for her to relocate from Colorado to Key West. Our parents had died in a car accident and there was no reason for her to return to the Samoan islands. But, she met someone on campus. She didn't realize it until it was too late, but her new boyfriend was a heroin addict. She started using. I put her in treatment programs a few times, but she never stayed. Six years ago, she called and said she wanted help getting clean. I flew to Denver, got to her place, and found her coming down off a high. We argued, and then...it happened so fast. She ran. I tried to stop her. She grabbed the knife from the block and lunged for me. I saw the blade. Knew I had failed her. When the tip pierced my skin, the knowledge that I hadn't protected her, hurt worse than the actual jagged cut."

"No, no..." Tori plead. "You tried to save her. Somewhere inside she knew you loved her. What happened next?"

"She called an ambulance, and then overdosed herself on heroin before they arrived. She took care of me, staunched the bleeding until the paramedics got there. Guess she remembered some of the things I'd taught her during my training."

"Oh God."

"She died in my arms." He squeezed Tori harder. Neither of them spoke for long seconds. "Teuila would've liked you."

"I'm so sorry, Trace."

Her voice held genuine regret at his loss, but not pity.

It didn't hurt so much to talk about it now. Teuila was in a better place and so was he. Tori made him want to live again.

Trace captured her face between his palms. "I want you to stay."

Her smile slipped. He expected her to say something, but instead caught the glimpse of fear that crossed her face. Trace sat up and pulled her onto his lap.

"Tell me right now why you can't stay with me?"

"Trace you don't know what you're asking for. The trouble that's coming for me won't hesitate to destroy you. My leaving is for the both of us."

He raised up onto his elbow to stare down at her.

"Help me to understand your logic because I'm confused as hell." He tried to control his anger. She had feelings for him, but she was too scared to explore the possibility of their future together.

"You want to be here with me?"

He narrowed his eyes at her when it looked like she would try and deny she had feelings for him. He wouldn't allow her to leave his arms without some answers to where they were headed.

"I do. Being in your arms, having the chance to know love with you means the world to me, but..."

"You won't stay because of this," he said yanking her arm up to reveal the track marks.

Frustration reigned in his head. He knew how junkies behaved. Had lived the cruel reality of having a drug addict in his life. Tori's story was somehow different.

For once, she pulled her arm back.

"I'm not a junkie. Only thing remotely suspicious in

my background is I pawned my mother's ruby rose pendant to buy my bus ticket here and get a few things."

He knew that without her telling him, but when she didn't say anything more, he snapped.

"Who did this to you?"

The defiance he was accustomed to from her drained away.

"Let's just say my guardian has friends with prescriptive authority."

"Oh." Trace frowned. A reputable healthcare provider would never ravage her flesh and cause the damage that was evident on Tori. No, the scars he saw were the physical evidence of sadistic brutality and neglect.

"Why?" he growled.

"Look, it's a past best left unspoken. You don't have to look at them."

"But, you like to, don't you?" He'd noticed her staring at her scarred arms more than once. A few times he'd watched as she idly rubbed over the marks, like she could erase them. "You're comfortable with people seeing your scars."

She didn't want to hide. Yet, she was in hiding. He knew it with every fiber of his being. She didn't trust him to help her. No woman should ever be terrified of a man she trusted or one that would take advantage of her trust.

She glanced down at her arms and shrugged. "They remind me that there are demons in this world. Demons that unleash something in you that you never knew existed."

"Does this demon have a name?"

She sucked her bottom lip between her teeth. When she spoke next, he could hear the unease lacing her words. "Like would be a poor choice of words to describe how I feel about my birth marks."

So, she wasn't going to give him a name.

"Birth marks?" No one came out of the womb with stenciled arms like hers.

"What I went through gave birth to a different woman."

"You trust me with your body, but not your safekeeping?"

"After what I've suffered, surrendering my body to you last night was safekeeping personified, Trace."

The sadness reflected in her eyes told him more than he wanted to know about their situation. They didn't have much time left.

She tried to scramble off his lap, but he stopped her. "Talk."

"You know I'm a little impulsive. He believes I need *help* to control my behavior."

"And his name is?" Trace pressed again.

"Denton Drake, but his name doesn't matter. My father is the key. My mother died of a ruptured aneurysm when I was seventeen. Nine months later, my father suffered a second heart attack. Denton was there for both of us. Father trusted Denton with his very life," she stammered, "and mine."

"How so?"

"My father added a marriage stipulation to my trust. On my twenty-fifth birthday, if I'm married, I'll gain access to my trust and fifty percent of my father's company. Denton manipulated my father into surrendering control of the company to him. He hired a team of physicians to manage my father's care. They kept him drugged and when I tried to help, they...they–let's just say Denton can be very convincing."

She didn't have to finish the sentence. He rubbed at the scars on her arms.

"He had you drugged." Fury ignited in Trace's blood, but when she began to tremble he tightened his arm around her hips and pulled her closer, wishing he could have been there to protect her.

She nodded. "Six months with only my silent screams. No control over who looked at me, who touched me, the voices surrounding me."

She was watching for his reaction, but Trace didn't blame her for any of it. Denton Drake had taken advantage of a young girl mourning her mother. Her tormenter would feel his wrath. He looked at his woman. In Tori's eyes, Trace would be powerless to stop the man coming for her. But, she was wrong.

"With Denton at the helm, the both of you will have to share power?" Trace questioned.

"That's not exactly how it'll work."

Trace rolled on top of her. "Tell me everything," he growled. She was censoring the information. Why would another man coming to take her away not matter?

"Because I agreed to marry him."

Trace stiffened, and then he took a deep inhale, consciously ordering his muscles to relax. "Huh."

She looked up, eyes wide. "You're not upset with me?"

He leaned forward, placing a kiss on her forehead.

He gave a sly grin. "No, Princess, I'm not upset."

"Why aren't you more," she waved her hands in the air, "manic about my being engaged?"

"Because, that shit ain't gonna happen." He shifted his hips, simultaneously spreading her legs wide to receive him.

"There's more."

"I'm all ears, Princess."

"My birthday is the day after tomorrow."

"We'll have to start the celebration early because I'm on rotation tomorrow night."

"You're really not bothered by all this?"

Odd, he felt a kindred spirit in Tori. Teuila was his only family. It left him raw that he wasn't able to keep the predators at bay, giving her a chance to experience life. Somehow, through that stab wound, he'd traded places with her. Imprisoning himself in guilt and shame, he become addicted to this internal pain. When the anger at Teuila, and at his failure finally surfaced, coupled with the nightmares of her charging at him with that knife aimed at his heart, he'd turned the sense of betrayal inward. Better to bear the burden in silence than to tarnish his sister's memory. They'd only had each other. Trace had been the oldest. It had been his responsibility to get her some place safe, keep her clean. No matter how many times she'd walked away, he should have followed. He wouldn't repeat his mistake.

"I'm bothered that you think you have to leave me." He kissed her. "Let me worry about Denton. After breakfast," he winked, "I'll drive you down to Hobo Alley for that job."

With him on duty overnight, Rachel would keep an eye on Tori. He'd talk with Kendall about her Grandmother Dinah and her housemate, Mrs. Elliott keeping Tori close by in the evenings.

"You've changed your mind?"

"Something like that." Nathan and Cutler would have to be in the loop. Not much happened in town without those two knowing something about it. "You stay with me and I'll take care of you." He tucked her head beneath his chin. Where she would stay.

❖

Tori grabbed another order from the end of the bar and loaded her tray. Trace had driven her to work and proceeded to stand guard at the bar. He was serious about her not leaving his sight. If a guy even smiled at her, he was flexing like a muscle head on an ego trip. Claudia had returned to work. The competition that Tori had anticipated from the seasoned waitress was unfounded.

Claudia had welcomed her with open arms.

When there was a lull in the Saturday afternoon crowd, Claudia led them out the rear entrance to the small storeroom and employee lounge behind the bar. She was grateful for the break. Tori's voice was hoarse from talking over the jukebox. The first drunk of the day had knocked a tray from Tori's portering arm and stepped on her toes. The space was little more than a prefabricated utility shed with metal shelves lining one wall and four wooden tables for counting inventory. The information extraction session started immediately.

"So, what's going on with you and Trace?"

Claudia's natural blonde curls courtesy of #10NB were piled high on her head. It reminded Tori of a beehive. There were rhinestones embedded in her hot pink manicure. She wore the signature black Hobo Alley t-shirt except she'd added a rhinestone pendant with the words 'high class' in all capital letters where her name tag should have been.

Tori was grateful that the question focused on Trace and not her. So far, no one had asked her about her last name or where she was from. Rachel hadn't questioned her when she asked to be paid in cash. She figured they thought she was on the run from a crazy ex-boyfriend or something. And that was kind of the truth. Denton needed her to seize complete control. With the money in her trust and control of her company shares, she would be at his mercy. Even if she managed to escape again, he had her father. This was her last chance to save her father. They would run fast, hard, and far. But Denton had the Currey family resources to locate them as long as her father was incapacitated. Plus, he knew eventually she'd have to contact her father. All he really had to do was wait her out. Without any money or friends she could trust, she was on her own, except for Trace.

"Trace and I are getting to know one another."

"Oh, yeah." She grinned. "Is he any good at it?"

Tori's mouth fell open. The corners of the older woman's eyes crinkled.

"I don't kiss and tell."

Claudia laughed out right. "Leave out the kissing parts and get to the juicy stuff," the woman said sinking down onto her elbow.

Tori sobered. Why was the woman interested in the details of her and Trace? Had Denton gotten to her. She'd learned that everyone had a price, even those who'd taken an oath to do no harm.

Claudia drew back and regarded the frown Tori knew

covered her face. "Slow down, Tori. I'm no threat. It's just that Trace is kind of mysterious. After everything that went down out west, he keeps to himself. You're the first woman he's ever brought in the place. I'm just a nosey lady. Not interested in a cat fight with a twenty-year old."

"Twenty-four-year-old," she corrected.

"Oh, so you're younger than his–" Claudia stopped talking.

Tori flipped her hair out of her face, rolling her shoulders to release the tension. "I know about Teuila. But, I've never asked Trace his age."

When she'd awoke to find him at her bedside, renewed hope fired to life deep inside. His voice, those dark eyes, and his name had sandblasted themselves into her memory. For her, Trace would remain ageless. He'd given her the fairytale dream with their night together.

"Get it, girlie. The sex must be amazing if you haven't even asked the man's age." Claudia slapped her knee. Her eyes dazzled with the nugget of information she'd gleaned. "He's thirty-one, by the way."

With a satisfied smile, the waitress sauntered off. The cellphone Trace had picked up for her on the way to Hobo Alley chimed. It was a text message from him.

She read it. *Why don't I see you?*

She replied. *Seek and ye shall find the newest employee.*

A minute later the door marked 'STAFF ONLY' burst open. Trace dressed in a black t-shirt, black jeans, and black boots strode through, sucking up all the oxygen, first out of the room, and then her lungs.

He lifted a brow, questioning why she was hanging in the back room alone.

She crooked a finger, beckoning him forward. "Waiting for you." She grinned.

When he reached her, he swatted her bottom. "Next time call first. No vanishing acts. I have seven o'clock reservations for two."

When he waggled his brows, she started shaking her head, though she couldn't stop giggling.

"No hanky panky allowed in the storeroom. I need this job."

Tori opened her arms to him.

"You need me, more."

Never had it been this way. Her father had kept her under lock and key until Denton came along. At first, he'd seemed to genuinely care for her, but it had been an act. What she had with Trace was real. Before Trace, she never would've believed in love at first sight. But from the moment she'd opened her eyes, seen him walking out the door, she knew she wanted him. Now she knew, she loved him. Trace let her embrace him, and then he lifted her off her feet.

"True." Gosh, if she let him. he'd keep her feet off the ground. Who knew a man could feel so good in her arms?

Tori reached up, ready to kiss Trace senseless. A crash sounded at his back, and then a tower of glasses careened toward the cement floor.

Tori screamed. Two men with extended batons stood in the doorway. Both were focused on her. The one on the right was average height. He sported a graying ponytail and thick arms, but he was too wide to be considered athletic. Maybe he worked as a meaty bouncer at a hillbilly bar. The guy on the left had a scar over his left eye that looked fresh and a nose that probably looked better broken. This one looked as if he could give and take some damage.

Trace growled low in his throat. "Both of you, get out of here."

Both men grinned. Tori recoiled at the array of broken and missing teeth between the pair. Instant concern for Trace overwhelmed her. She had a feeling if she agreed to go with them, Trace would still bear their calling card.

Scar spoke up. "Give us the girl and we won't hurt you too bad."

Trace took a step forward. With a hand behind his back he motioned for her to stay.

Facing the men, he gave a harsh laugh. "I'm going to give you twin concussions."

Meaty lunged for her. Truly, she had no idea how he moved so fast. In a synchronized move, Scar attacked Trace. Instincts kicking in, Tori scrambled through the maze of tables while keeping an eye on Trace. If she ran fast enough, maybe she could beat Meaty to the storeroom door, but she couldn't leave Trace.

From the corner of her eye, she glanced in Trace's direction. Tori's mouth fell open. Trace had dropped low into a fighting stance. Before she could warn him not to risk injury, he moved in a lightning fast circular movement. His leg shot out. Scar came up off his feet before falling backwards. His head struck the door. A crunchy thwack sounded. Tori's eyes widened. That move. She'd seen Lima Lama techniques before, but she never imagined Trace practiced Samoan marital arts. His fluid grace and strength was a deadly dance that riveted her.

Beefy hands clipped her waist, the motion sending her torso full speed ahead.

"Get your hands off me, meat head. My boyfriend is going to break your stupid face." Arms raised over her head, Tori used her hands to tear at his hair. The more he thrashed the harder she pulled, until strands broke free.

"Ouch...you witch."

A whole lot scared and a little enraged, Tori threw her head back and nailed him in the mouth. He yelled out and smacked her lower leg hard with the baton.

A swift and penetrating pain gripped her. She cried out as her legs crumpled beneath her.

"Get up or I'll hit you again," he drawled.

In the throes of pain, Tori struggled to focus. From somewhere in the room a roar vibrated the very air. It felt as if her teeth rattled in her skull. Suddenly, the arm around her waist was ripped away. Trace pushed her clear of Meaty as he charged forward, the menace rolling off him, crowding the small space. He was on the guy before Tori could take in a breath.

"You hit her," Trace bellowed before plowing his fist into Meaty's nose. Blood splattered his knuckles, but he didn't stop there. No, Tori watched in horror as the beast Trace kept on a leash, broke free, and pummeled Meaty to the ground. What had she done to him?

✛

Fear ripped through Tori. Denton's goons had found her, yes. But, Trace had transformed before her eyes. The man who'd read her romance novels, cooked her dinner, loved her with a gentleness she didn't think possible, had disappeared. She blinked several times, but there was no use. The human carnage surrounded her.

"Trace," her voice a broken whisper, "I'm okay. I'm alright," she said as tears gathered in her eyes. Trace's huge body straddled Meaty. His beautiful mane hung in wild chunks around his head. His nostrils flared like an angry pit bull. His knuckles were raw and swollen. Meaty had stopped fighting, but like a predator with a fresh scent in his nose, Trace didn't want to let go. He maintained a stance of dominance, his posture flexed and ready, daring anyone take his prize.

She wrapped both her arms around his biceps. Dear heaven, he was strong. In the recesses of her mind, she wished a bald man in a plastic wheelchair and his dork hat sidekick would appear to stop the destruction she'd wrought to Trace and Rachel. Her heart broke with each blow he delivered. She pictured him with Teuila, wanting to save her, each powerful fist disintegrating the heroin, the failed therapies, and the blade.

"Trace, baby." The endearment got his attention. His head popped up. She took the opening, turning his face, until their eyes met. "Your Tori is okay."

Pounding footsteps were headed in their directions, the chorus of voices rising in the small space. The door opening, voices were coming from all around them. Cursing, a few gasps, a sob that sounded like Claudia, maybe Rachel. Trace didn't move and neither did she. Trace had come to her rescue, but the way he tore into that guy, all the blood on his hands made her think he was on his way to a jail cell. Funny, her first thought was she'd go with him. For a woman who'd spent six months locked in her body, being caged behind bars with Trace sent a zing of excitement through her.

"Trace?" It was Nathan.

"Oh, man," another voice called. Tori kept her eyes on Trace. Now Nathan held one arm and Cutler was on the other side.

Nathan tugged at Trace's arm. "Come on big guy. We've got you."

His bicep and the muscles along his forearm strained as he pulled against Trace's larger mass. Cutler struggled in an equally tense pose.

Commanding Fire

A tall young guy with blond hair, striking blue eyes and a gold badge entered the melee. Someone had called the cops. There were at least nine people huddled at the door, looking in–their expressions grim. This could mean trouble for Trace. With a rising sense of panic, Tori's brain started to conjure an exit strategy for him.

"Cutler," the sheriff called out. "What happened here?"

"Ask her," someone said.

Trace, on his feet, shook off both his friends. Wincing, he wiped blood away from his mouth. His knuckles sported fresh bruises. The guy who'd hit her lay sprawled on the floor, but he was rolling from side to side. Teetering his flabby body into an upright position.

When the blond with the golden badge extended his hand to her, Trace snapped. "Don't touch her."

The storeroom occupants fell mute with chilled surprise. Trace had calmed, but aggression emanated from him. A few took a step back.

"Come here, Tori."

Instinctively, she knew he'd never hurt her. She walked into his open arms. He gripped her face between his hands.

"You okay?" he asked. He used his body to cage her

in. The smell of blood, coppery and sweet, mixed with natural wood scent and his masculine sweat. Determined to be the rock he'd been for her, Tori held him tight, until her heartbeat melded with his. He'd shed blood to protect her. And, this was just the beginning if she chose to stay.

She nodded. Her rapid heartbeat calmed when he pressed his lips to her forehead. Everything had happened so quickly. The two men, the batons, Meaty grabbing her, and Trace's choreographed response. And Trace had put both men down…for her. Pride and…love slammed into her like a mega yacht. Tori luxuriated in the fact that an honorable man would risk his safety for hers. Nestling in closer, she let loose the sob from her throat.

"Shh, Princess. I've got you."

But, who had him? "Trace." Her voice broke. Tori inhaled a steady breath, reeling the emotion backward. She could be strong for Trace.

"Ma'am," the sheriff approached. "I'm Lance Stevens, with the Monroe County Sheriff's department. Can you tell me what happened?"

Sniffling, Tori looked to Trace, before she spoke. He nodded. She swallowed and explained what happened before the man grabbed her. She hadn't recognized either man, but she never did. Denton had a lot of people on his payroll. Anyone could be a threat.

Afterwards, Lance, who she discovered was Cutler's younger brother, thanked her for her statement. Trace remained at her side.

"You are free to go. I'll need your address and phone number," Lance stated, scribbling on his pad. "More questions may arise when we get him to the station." Lance motioned to the cuffed man still on the floor of the storeroom.

"Ah," she said looking to Trace. "What's our address and phone number?"

Lance stared from her to Trace. "You're staying at Trace's? Since when?"

"That's irrelevant," Trace cut in. Trace rattled off the address and phone number before she could memorize either. Was she that trusting of him that she hadn't bothered to memorize the address or ask him for the house phone number? He'd provided the information to the nurse for her discharge, but she had been anxious to get out the door before Denton located her.

She needed cash. Rachel approached them, worry lines etched across her forehead.

"Tori, I'm so sorry." Guilt laced the words. "Did he hurt you?" Tori thought to reassure her. Besides, the ache to her right thigh, she was no worse for the wear.

"I'm fine, but you could make it up to me," she said, giving Trace a sideways glance.

Trace frowned at her. The hand that lay on his chest vibrated from his gruff rumble.

"Anything," Rachel said.

"I need a loan."

"Yes."

"No."

The yes belonged to Rachel. Tori acted as if she hadn't heard Trace's no.

"Thank you, we can talk about it once I'm done here."

Trace picked her up bringing her face flush with his. "I said no."

She kissed his nose. "I heard you, sweetie. You've been out voted."

There were several chuckles, before she heard. "Oh, man. This will be fun to watch."

Tori looked at Trace's grim expression. She didn't want to upset him, but she needed her own money. How else could she get out of town fast? Victoria Currey's reality had arrived in brutal fashion. Being with Trace had been a fantasy. It was time for her to leave and create a new reality for herself. And maybe...returning to Trace would be a part of it...one day.

Chapter Nine

Trace found himself on the outside looking in as the vibrant woman he'd shared his home with locked down her emotions tighter than Fort Knox. Tori had been too quiet on the drive back to the golf course and he thought to cancel their birthday dinner celebration, but she'd insisted they go. Now, he was having second thoughts. He'd rocked the foundation of who she thought he was with his reaction to her being attacked. She sat across from him, her face buried in the wine menu. She could pass a wine sommelier class without having drank the stuff.

"I remember that you don't drink. Do you plan to start after today?"

She raised her head. A soft sigh on her lips. Lips he wanted to kiss. "No."

News of the altercation at Hobo Alley earlier in the day, and that he had a fire victim under his roof had reached the firehouse. Captain Brady had called for Trace to be in his office at eight o'clock sharp in the morning. He knew he was facing a possible reprimand, but Tori came first. Her zeal for life energized him. He wasn't about to lose the woman he cared about...loved. A wave of regret hit him that she'd witnessed the beast within, but he'd do it again, if it meant she was safe. It was only their second night together, yet it felt like they had shared a lifetime. How had he lived before her? He hadn't. After their initial conversations, he thought she was flighty and hyperactive, but neither was true. This morning she'd read the Wall Street Journal and made stock recommendations. She watched the Bloomberg report like she had millions invested in the market. When those two henchmen tried to take her, she'd fought back. As much as Trace believed she didn't owe him for saving her, he felt that since she was the catalyst for several of the changes in his life, she should have to stay around. A permanent investor in the project she'd started in him.

"Are you afraid...of me?" If it were anyone else, he'd welcome the separation. But not Tori, he had a hard limit with her trying to put distance between them.

She angled her head. He noticed she did that when she was thinking. "I'm afraid for what I've done to you. I've upset your pleasant life."

Trace scoffed. "I want you. Pleasant or unpleasant, I want what we have, Princess.

A tentative smile spread across her lips. "Really?"

He winked. "Yeah, really."

Abruptly she came to her feet. Was she leaving him? When she pulled at the seat closest to him with the window overlooking Whitehead Street, he breathed a sigh of relief. "Then let's get this celebration started because this is a nice restaurant, Trace."

The tension in his shoulders abated. This was his Tori. He looked around at the flowery decor and fancy wine bottles everywhere. If she wanted ritzy dinners and candlelight every night, he'd give it to her.

"Glad you like it. Too many flowers for my tastes. Speaking of which, your roses have turned their smile upside down."

"My flowers are not due for an upgrade, so paws off, Beastie. They stay until the last petal bites the dust. Now, back to my pre-birthday dinner. I love French food. I had no idea that you enjoyed their cuisine."

He didn't either. He'd asked Symphony and Kendall. They had recommended Pièd a Terre. Trace took one glance at the menu and slammed it shut. Everything was in French. Geez, he would be thoroughly embarrassed when it came time to order.

"If you don't like what's on the menu. I'll take you someplace else."

Preferably with a bed and a couple of silk ropes. Not

that he was into bondage, but he needed her complete surrender. Tori needed to stay with him. His time in Texas would go faster with her in his bed every night.

"No worries, Beastie. I'm not cheap, but I'm easy." She giggled, and then added. "To please. Besides, you can't go wrong with seafood on an island."

"True," he chuckled.

A card stock menu rose between them. Trace expected her to wince when she tried to read the thing. Instead, she scanned the entire thing with a critical eye. He waited for her to crack a joke.

The waiter approached. Trace opened his mouth, prepared to ask the suited gentleman for recommendations.

"S'il vous plait Monsieur," Tori interrupted.

The bow tied older man regarded Tori with a smile, a welcomed surprise obvious on his face. "Nous désirons en entrées les coquilles Saint Jacques à la noix do coco et au gingembre. Et le bar accompagné de riz au safran et petite légumes en plat principal. Il prendra une bière blonde de Key West et une bouteille d'eau pour moi. Merci."

Trace's mouth dropped open. A deep bow was rendered to them both before the happy man dashed off to place their orders. He narrowed his eyes on the woman smiling at him from across the table.

"You speak French?"

She nodded. "And Spanish and Chinese. Japanese is next on my list."

"You're amazing," he said meaning every word. "So, what am I eating, Princess?"

"Sea scallops in coconut and ginger for an appetizer. I ordered us the sea bass with saffron rice and baby vegetables."

Trace groaned in anticipation of the food hitting his taste buds with a giant splash.

"Sounds perfect," he said. A cold bottle of hops and barley would have been perfect to wash down all those fancy French spices. He wouldn't mention it. Not with his woman taking care of him with the meal. He could get back to basics when they got home.

"Glad you're happy. Your Key West Ale should be here soon." She winked and he couldn't help the smile that spread across his mug. "I think you're pretty fantastic too, Beastie."

She knew him too well. The realization pleased him, but not as much as when Tori leaned forward, deliberately sampling up her cleavage by pressing her arms along her ribcage. Trace treated himself to the view, marveling at the display made just for him.

"This night is almost perfect, Trace."

"Almost?"

"You know I have to put my spin on it," she said. A mischievous laugh escaped.

"What did you do?"

She leaned in conspiratorially. "What are your thoughts on women with no panties on?"

Beneath the table, Tori grabbed his hand and placed it on her bare thigh. Oh, so soft. Blood rushed to his sex, leaving him speechless. Her skin seemed to burn hotter as he slid his hand north, climbing the stairway to his own slice of heaven. When his fingers brushed damp curls, he gave her moist folds a gentle stroke. Tori gasped, his name on her lips. Trace forgot to think at all. He could get used to dessert first.

❖

Tori groaned when Trace's alarm blared the Norah Jones's *Come Away With Me*. Sunday mornings were supposed to be for quiet time cuddled on the couch with your lover.

"You sure you're going to be okay?" he frowned. Their gourmet dinner tasted like a dollar menu item compared to the dessert they had served each other until their sweat drenched bodies begged for sleep.

"Trace, you're going to work, not off to war. I'll be fine."

"I left money on the counter. My numbers are on the fridge." He'd shuffled her out of Hobo Alley before she and Rachel could settle their business dealings.

She kissed him. "You know you told me this last night."

"Yeah, well. You sleep hard. I need to make sure you remember."

"Call me before you leave for Symphony's. Kendall's grandmother will be there. She's a great cook. Save me a plate."

"Should I call on my bathroom breaks and when I get home, daddy?"

"Now you're getting the picture. Oh, I have a package being delivered today."

She laughed. "If I called as much as you asked, you'd never get any sleep."

He hauled her up close, settling a kiss on her forehead. "I'll sleep when I come home to you." She and Trace had discussed her staying. Symphony and friends had volunteered to play babysitter while he was on the clock.

Tori handed him his packed lunch for work. "Go," she said, walking him to the door. Alone, she grabbed her cell from the counter, and flopped on the couch. She eyed the counter. Her roses had all but died, but one rose, dark and crisp on the edges, clung to the stem. Maybe, tomorrow she'd shop for a fresh bouquet.

Something in her news feed caught her attention. Denton Drake, Chief Executive Officer of Currey Industries headed to Palm Beach for rest and relaxation. The bottom fell out of Tori's stomach. Denton...in Florida. She was sure the staff at the resort they owned in Palm Beach would provide him with an alibi. Tori needed to get to her father before Denton relocated him again. She'd have to get into the nursing home tonight. Denton hadn't sent more henchmen. He was coming for her. That was so much worse.

By seven o'clock, Tori had a plan. Trace had given her the keys to his truck while he caught a ride with Cutler to the station.

The first thing she did was to visit the airport locker that held her disguise. When she'd arrived on the Greyhound bus five days ago, she'd rented a locker at the island's single transportation hub to store her things. After the fire, Trace had provided for all her needs. There hadn't been a reason to return here, until today. Dressed in blue scrubs and Birkenstock shoes, Tori parked in the staff parking and entered the facility. She had to find her father before she was discovered. She didn't have a medical background if anyone asked her any questions, but she'd suffered at the hands of so called healers for the last six months, so she spoke their language. So intent on her plan, she missed the approaching fire department engine with Trace in the front seat.

✣

Trace hopped from the engine cab. Was that Tori who'd just entered the senior village? There was still another ninety minutes till sunset, but she should have been at Symphony's by now. Only one of the buildings had been destroyed in the fire. The residents had been relocated to another building on the property.

"Hold up, Trace." That was Kendall calling out behind him.

"I'll meet you inside," he said already moving toward the building.

Twice a year they partnered with the Red Cross to test

and install fire detectors for local residents. With all the seniors in temporary lodging, Captain Brady had directed them to test all the detectors in the common areas of the facility. Why was Tori here? Did she know one of the residents?

"Here," she said handing him a bag filled with battery operated detectors.

"The faster we get started, the faster we can get back to the station." Like most firefighters, Kendall lived for the flame. Community outreach was a part of the job, but running into the flames kept the adrenaline pumping in her veins.

Trace spotted Tori entering a bedroom on the first floor. He walked to the door and pushed it open, but he didn't enter. Tori sat on the bed beside an old man. He was drugged beyond consciousness laying with his eyes open, but fixed on the ceiling.

"Daddy, it's me, Victoria."

Victoria. The name suited her, though she'd always be his Tori.

"Daddy," she said again softly. "You've got to fight the pull of the drug. It's your little spark plug...Daddy, please."

When he just lay there. The organ in the middle of

Trace's chest ached for his woman. His eyes narrowed when Tori withdrew a small vial and a syringe. She expertly drew the liquid from the glass bottle and injected the man's thin arm. So, she had a bag stashed somewhere else. Trace searched his emotional closet. Was he angry at her deception? No, he was impressed with her ingenuity. Knowing Tori, she used some of the pawn money to buy a drug reversal agent. She had anticipated her father's condition. He really did love this remarkable creature who'd risked her safety for her father, for him.

The old man's eyes fluttered and slowly focused. His gaze wandered before landing on his daughter.

"Tori," he whispered. "Is it really you?"

"Yes," she sobbed.

Her father's eyes roved over her face before he surveyed her arms. "Oh no." Her father's voice began to quake, "he got to you, too."

"Shh, I'm okay. I got away, but..."

Tears streamed down wrinkled cheeks. "I thought I was protecting you. Thought he appreciated how special you are... would help you once I'm gone."

"He's coming for me, Daddy."

Trace had heard enough. Denton Drake would pay for preying on Tori and her father.

"Don't let him get his hands on you again," the old man warned, and then he smiled. "I was wrong to think you couldn't run the company by yourself. Go now, my little spark plug."

"I can't leave you here, Daddy. They'll keep you a prisoner."

"Think about yourself for once, Victoria. I've lived my life, no matter what—"

"Who are you?"

Trace spun around to find a man dressed in gray slacks and a lab coat. He spoke loud enough for Tori to hear him. "Name's Trace Fletcher. Me and my partner are on scene checking the smoke detectors."

"Oh." The man relaxed. "I can direct you to all the units on this floor. Please come with me."

"I need to check these rooms, too."

"I'm sorry the patients in this wing are not to be disturbed.

Trace would be back for answers and he'd create quite the disturbance if anyone tried to stop him.

❖

Tori needed to return Trace's truck. The Key West

firehouse was packed with engines and ladder trucks. Loud hip hop, country, and soft rock thrummed through the air from every direction. She knew he wasn't at the station because she'd heard his voice outside of her father's room. How much of their conversation had he overheard? After leaving the senior village, Tori had driven to Hobo Alley. Claudia had followed her to the firehouse and was waiting for her in the car. Tori had saved enough money to rent a car for her and her father. All she had to do was drop off the keys to Trace's truck, catch a lift back to the rental car agency, and then pick up a few things from the townhouse.

"Hey, Tori." He spoke loud enough to be heard over the radio chorus that didn't seem to bother anyone but her.

Nathan stared at her with his assessing gray eyes. She bet it was impossible to mislead the man. It seemed as if he looked right through her.

"Ah, I...could you point me in the direction of Trace's locker."

A golden lab came up beside him and dropped down on its haunches.

"Who's this fella?" she asked, stroking the dog's head.

"This is Max. He's my partner."

Max eager for more attention circled her legs, rubbing

his head on her shins.

"Cool," she said, not meeting his eyes. "Ah... so, where's his locker?"

"Tori."

She could tell by his solemn tone that getting the answer wouldn't be an easy feat.

She sighed, and looked up regarding Nathan's rugged features. "Look, I'm kind of in a hurry. If you're not going to answer my question, tell me who I need to speak with and I'll be on my way."

"Trace won't like it if you disappear on him."

Great, Nathan was going to make her decision to leave harder. If she could preserve what she and Trace had, and keep herself and her father out of Denton's claws, she would do it. But, given the condition her father was in, Denton had rendered them both powerless to stop his takeover. On paper, her father had given him command and control. The only thing he needed to solidify his permanent position as the head of Currey Industries was her name on a marriage license.

"I won't either."

Nathan inhaled a breath, and then rolled his shoulders up and back as if he were unloading a heavy weight.

"So, you're in to him, too?"

"In too deep," she said in truth. Trace was the kind of man that made it hard for a woman to resist. He was the steady force she'd been looking for her entire life. There was nothing fake about the man. He liked his life orderly, yet he made room for her before he even knew her name. She loved him and she would stay with him forever if given the opportunity.

"Then stay."

She shook her head. Nathan didn't understand what was at stake. Denton would lock her mind and her body in a chemical cell. The people in his employ answered only to him. He replaced all the employees and staff loyal to her family with his henchman. They ruthlessly executed his orders. No one could stop them.

Recognizing that Nathan would not assist her, she pulled the keys from her back pocket. "Give him these from me, will you?"

Nathan glanced at the keys, but he didn't reach for them.

After a moment, Tori released the keys expecting them to clink against the cement slab at any moment. Nathan caught them mid-air.

"You sure about this, Tori. We'll help with whoever has you on the run."

Her gaze shot from the keys in his grasp to his face. He smirked.

"I know a few things about a woman in trouble. My Symphony had some trouble when she first came to town."

Tori snorted. "My kind of trouble will get Trace hurt."

Nathan grinned. "Give Trace a chance to slay your dragons, darling. You'd be surprised at the extent of his reach.

"Good bye, Nathan. Tell Trace not to come looking for me." She pulled the pamphlet for the waist of her jeans. The leaflet detailed all the information of the corporation and she'd added a copy of her trust including her father's stipulation regarding her marriage. "He'll understand once he reads this."

Nathan shook his head. "No, he won't."

Tori turned to leave. He had to believe her leaving would be the safest thing for her and for Trace. If Denton were targeting Trace, it would destroy her.

Chapter Ten

Trace returned to the station, but only to clock out. Engine 10 was parked in the first bay, so he hadn't missed any call outs. Good. He needed to find Tori. He'd called her cell phone several times, each call had gone to voice mail.

Nathan waved him over, but Trace climbed the stairs to Chief Brady's office.

"Trace, hold up," Nathan called out.

Trace shot a sharp look at his friend. "Later," he ground out.

"No...now."

The hairs on the back of Trace's neck came to attention. Nathan's voice held an edge that had him slowing his pace.

"What?" he asked, caution separating each syllable.

"Tori."

The one word had Trace turning and trotting back down the stairs.

The door behind Trace opened. He spun around. Captain Brady stood in his office doorway, his thinning hair plastered to his scalp.

"Fletcher," he bellowed. "The senior village administer is on the phone threatening to file a complaint against the station for a disruption caused by one, or both of my firefighters. Get in here right now, and enlighten me as to how you've added another swinging weight to my jock strap."

"Can't now, Captain. I need to leave."

The Captain raked a hand through thin strands of gray hair. "Trace, I didn't ask. You and Kendall had the staff evacuate the entire facility for a mock fire drill," the Captain's voice climbed above a three-alarm fire. "This doesn't look good."

Trace crossed his arms over his chest. "I don't care what it looks like."

"Your attitude isn't helping your case, Fletcher."

"Never said it would."

The Captain threw up his hands. "What the heck is going on in this station?"

He hit Trace with a hard stare. "You've got ten minutes to get your head out of your hidey hole and get in my office," the Captain said, returning to his office.

"Don't need it. I'll be gone in less than five." Trace focused on Nathan. "What about, Tori?"

"Your future," the Captain tossed over his shoulder.

Yeah, Trace's future was with Tori. He could find another job if necessary, but he couldn't lose the woman he loved. He wouldn't.

Nathan pulled a set of keys from his uniform pocket. Trace knew instantly they were his. "How long she been gone?"

"Maybe forty-minutes and Trace...she's scared."

Trace pulled at his braid in frustration. "Damn it," he swore, kicking the tire on the engine closest to him. "I can take care of her."

"Your truck is parked out back. She left with Claudia in that beat up jalopy."

"She's going to make a run for it."

"Yup. I figured as much. How you want to handle this?"

"I need your help moving something."

Nathan frowned, but he followed him outside to the engine Trace and Kendall had driven.

When Trace opened the rear door, Nathan sucked in a breath.

"Well, that explains why you and Kendall staged a sunset fire drill. Who the hell is he?"

"Alfred Van Currey. Tori's father."

✣

Tori had her bag packed and on her shoulder when the doorbell rang. Had she left something in Claudia's car? No, it must be the package Trace told her to expect before he'd left for work. Tori bounded down the stairs and opened the door.

"Victoria?" The timbre of his voice brought a quiver to her insides, but she refused to allow him to see her fear. The wind had picked up strength since she'd returned to the townhouse. Tendrils of her hair whipped in front of her face. Interesting, the same wind seemed to steer clear of the man before her. Nothing moved, not even a rustle of his shirt. How appropriate. Denton Drake loved the control the medications gave him over her. He didn't fair too well when she was full strength. Even still, her heart beat so fast she thought she might pass out.

Denton had changed in the week she'd been away from him. With the blank look in his steely eyes, he looked more sinister than she remembered. Or maybe, compared to the love and kindness she'd had with Trace, his evil deeds seemed all the more wicked. He was lean, clean cut, with short dark hair perfectly in place. He looked like a Wall Street yuppie, fresh faced and eager to please. In reality, he was a cruel man who got off on mastering other people, with or without their consent.

"Denton."

He angled his head at the bag on her shoulder.

"Going somewhere?"

She tightened her grip on the bag.

"Actually, I was just leaving."

He smiled. "I hope it's to come back home to me."

Tori buried the smirk raring to show, not wanting to anger him. "Denton, please. Let me go."

"Tori," he said, his voice dripping with condescension. "Your father entrusted your care and welfare to me, and me alone."

"Well, we both know that was a mistake," she snapped.

The second the words left her mouth she realized her mistake. Control the impulses, Tori.

The friendly smile of patience fell away. "You've wasted enough of my time, Victoria. I can see now that your medication needs to be adjusted if you are to mind your behavior."

At the reminder that he would drug her again,

Tori struck out with her foot, clipping him on the knee. When he buckled. She spun on her other heel, sprinting to the rear porch. Denton recovered quickly. He pushed through the still open door and grabbed for her. His hand caught on the strap of her travel bag. Tori shrugged the luggage off her shoulder and bolted though the slider, leaped the fence, and ran across the golf cart path.

"Help me," she screamed. It was too late for anyone to be on the course. There were townhouses flanking the course, maybe someone would hear her.

"Victoria," Denton screamed, but then silence competed with the still of the night. She could hear cars entering the community through the manned security entrance. How had Denton gotten in? No doubt he'd bribed the guard, or the guy was already on the payroll. Tori took a shortcut through a wooded area. If she reached the guardhouse, she could call for help. She had to reach her father. If Denton relocated him again, she may never find him again, then she truly would be alone. She could see the motion lights surrounding the guardhouse in the distance. She looked left and right, before stepping into the clearing. Only one more path to cross before she would be safe. Tori took a step onto the path, and a shadow came from her left. She turned away, but the needle struck her upper arm, and penetrated deep before she could dodge.

"Go to sleep, Victoria." Denton said, as his arm snaked around her waist.

Instantly, her surroundings went fuzzy, and then blackness made the slow advance into her vision.

"Trace," she whispered, as her breathing slowed and her vision grew dim. She could feel the loss of control in her legs as she struggled to support her weight.

Denton laughed. "Trace won't find you, sweetheart. Even if he does, you'll be my wife by midnight."

A single tear escaped as her eyes closed. Denton would make it impossible for her to escape this time. Her final thought was of her hands buried in Trace's hair, her body nestled in close to his warmth. As the weightless sensation spread throughout her muscles, the drug rendered her a life-sided doll. Tori lost the fight as the fog engulfed what had been, and now only a blank canvas remained. The opioid leash brought her under Denton's command once more. This time she welcomed the paralysis, to stay in this barren place. But then something happened that had never happened before. Trace appeared to her through the fog. She reached for him. When he pulled her into his embrace, she fell asleep in her lover's arms.

❖

Trace walked to his open door. He heart pounded in his chest. Entering his home, the first thing he saw was Tori's V. Bradley bag on the floor. His mouth went dry, but he called for her despite knowing he wouldn't get an answer. The house no longer scented of roses. On the counter, all the rose stems were aged and withered in the vase, except one. A single pedal clung to the stalk. Trace tore his eyes away.

"Tori?"

Lance had followed him inside. "Looks like she left in a hurry," he said pointing to the open slider door leading to the backyard.

"She wouldn't leave out the back door."

Lance grunted and Trace knew what he was thinking. She wouldn't tear out the back unless someone prevented her from leaving via the front door. Why hadn't she gone to Symphony's? Trace huffed out a breath filled with fear and frustration.

A hand landed on his shoulder. "We'll find her."

Lance's voice held no pity, just a calm confidence. Trace had no doubt they would, but what condition would she be in if Denton had her. Her father could barely keep his eyes open, even though he hadn't been dosed with a sedative in a few hours. According to Alfred's medical records, his private staff was responsible for adhering to the physician's medication regimen, without oversight from the senior village staff. A dosing schedule that had kept him too doped up to provide care for himself or rescue his daughter from a madman. During the drive home, Trace had skimmed the papers Tori had left for him at the station. Her father had drafted an airtight contract to ensure his company and Tori were well taken care of. Unfortunately, even with her business degree, her father had predicated much of her company involvement on Tori having a counter balance in the form of a husband. Trace had two hours to reclaim his future with the woman he loved and the Currey legacy. When she married, Tori and her husband would control fifty percent of the company and her father the other fifty percent. With Denton controlling her father's share and the marriage granting him access to Tori's holdings, the interloper would effectively control one hundred percent of the Currey family business.

"Tori would head for other people. We'll check with the guard on the way out."

Chapter Eleven

Trace watched as Lance made call after call from his home phone. Gosh, his place felt huge without Tori, yet the weight of the walls seemed to press in on him. He ripped the tie from his hair, impatient to get some type of lead on Tori's whereabouts. The security guard confessed to hearing what could have been a scream, but admitted he thought it was kids playing on the course.

Lance put down the phone and faced him.

"Anything?"

Lance shook his head. "Patrol cars are looking for anything suspicious, but..."

Trace knew the drill. They didn't have enough information on Tori or Denton Drake. He could have taken her off the island, but Trace didn't think so. A businessman, like Drake, would want to secure the deal. Without a bead on Tori's father, that meant a loose end needed to be tied up.

"Trace, it's not looking good."

Trace extended his hand, appreciating that Lance had gone out on a limb for him. He didn't have any proof that Tori had been held against her will. Lance had seen her arms and the story of a reputable man keeping a woman a prisoner in her own home seemed far-fetched. He knew how it sounded.

"Thanks for everything."

"I'll keep my ear to the wall. If I hear—"

Trace interrupted, not wanting Lance to think he wasn't grateful for his help. "Appreciate it. I'll walk you out."

Just as they reached the door there was a knock. Trace grabbed the knob and pulled it wide. Cutler and Nathan stood with Max waggling his tail.

"What's going on?"

Nathan met his eyes. "Her dad is settled with Kendall and Symphony."

Trace lifted his hand in protest. No way did he want Nathan's pregnant wife and Kendall's itchy trigger finger responsible for Tori's dad.

"Don't worry," Cutler chimed in. "Adam has Symphony in hand and Shaky will make sure my girl doesn't put a bullet in anyone before it's time. Dinah and Mrs. Elliott have fed him twice, already."

After surviving an abusive marriage, Kendall was never far away from a weapon.

Lance walked out the door like he hadn't just

heard his brother discussing vigilante justice.

Trace was concerned that his friends may be in over their heads. They both had women they loved in their lives and he knew that if they followed him, it would lead to danger.

"You two sure you want to do this?"

Max barked his answer before either man responded.

"She's yours, right?" Nathan asked.

Trace nodded, "Tori's mine. And, I will get her back."

Anger and fear rose inside of him, thinking what Denton must have done to take her. Tori took care of everything she valued. She wouldn't have left their home unlocked because their slice of paradise meant everything to her. He knew she loved their home and him as sure as the breath entering his body.

"We'll help you bring your woman home."

Trace stepped aside, and his two best friends walked in. "I think she left us a trail."

Cutler narrowed his eyes on Trace. "How?"

Trace pulled the papers Tori had left for him at the station. The brochure had a list of all the private holdings of Currey Industries. "These highlighted properties," Trace began, "are in Key West." Damn, his woman was smart. Hang on, Princess. Trace would find her.

✤

Tori awoke on a large bed. She lay sprawled on her back. Someone had covered her in an oversized pullover shirt. Fresh cut flowers, lots of them were close by, though she didn't see any display vases. Denton knew her too well. The room was well appointed with floor to ceiling silk drapes, antique furniture, and a large baroque mirror facing the bed. Glancing at the watch affixed to her wrist, she realized only a few hours had passed. Denton must have been in a hurry. In the past, he removed all anchors to time, one day ran into the others. As she mentally flipped through all the locations he could have taken her in the elapsed time, one of the images from the brochure she'd left for Trace came to mind. She was in Currey Cove. The foundation owned a private island about one half mile off the Key West Coast. It might as well have been a thousand miles. There was no way to arrive on the island without announcing your arrival. Corporate owned all the vessels that traveled between the waterfront and the cove dock. Denton would never allow Trace to reach her.

"I'm glad that you are awake." The room light clicked on and Tori covered her eyes. Denton was not alone. A woman with a garment bag waited until he motioned her forward. "Good our guests will arrive within the hour."

"What guests?"

"Come, my darling. The wedding of the decade has to be witnessed, now get undressed."

Tori recoiled. "No."

The woman halted in her steps. Her eyes darted to Tori's. Tori forced herself not to look away. Would this woman help her? Denton cleared his throat. Instantly, the woman's gaze dropped to her feet. Inside Tori deflated, but she could not show any weakness in front of Denton. She had no doubt he would exploit any crack in her armor to his advantage.

"Get out of that bed, Tori."

She didn't move. He gave her a sinister grin before he reached into his pocket and withdrew another syringe. He didn't speak. There was no need. The drug spoke volumes. Tori snapped the duvet from over her legs. As if he wasn't in the room, she removed her outer shirt. The gasp from the seamstress should have alarmed her, but it didn't. Trace was the only person that had looked upon her shame without flinching. Trace, and the monster that had put those marks on her body, branding her with a lie.

"Happy now," she smirked, stepping out of her jeans.

"Very. I'm about to be the sole owner of a multi-billion-dollar company."

He snapped his fingers. "Get her ready," he demanded of the woman who was little more than a nuisance to him.

"Yes, sir."

Denton didn't acknowledge her reply.

"You won't get away with this," Tori sneered.

Denton raked his gaze over her disrobed body, lust gleaming in his eyes. "Who's going to stop me?"

Tori steeled her spine, refusing to back down from her statement. "Trace is going to rip you apart."

Tori hoped he'd looked through the copies of her trust and the Currey Family holdings. She hadn't known which move Denton would make, but the fact that she'd be twenty-five in less than two hours, she'd known they both were running out of time. She and

Denton were both in the race of their lives. Fortunately for her, Trace wouldn't stop until her found her. Would he get to her before the clock struck midnight?

Chapter Twelve

Trace stormed into Hobo Alley, furious as a summer storm. For once, silence greeted him. No jukebox, no rowdy tourists. Yet, a loud pounding sound rattled the teeth in his skull. He realized it was his brain cycling through facts and figures in overdrive. With Lance's help, they'd checked on every property on Tori's list. She wasn't at any of them.

"Damn it. Where could he have taken her?"

Rachel came over, three beers in hand. She sat an icy bottle in front of each of them.

Trace softly cursed. "It's eleven o'clock. He has to be setting up a ceremony somewhere." He dropped the contents of his hands on the tabletop. What was he missing? Every highlighted location had turned up a big fat zero.

Claudia walked over to their table, a grim expression on her face. She patted Trace on the shoulder. "You'll find her."

He was beginning to think Tori would be lost to him if he didn't reach her by midnight. Unless Denton flew in his own minister, Tori would have to be conscious for the wedding. But afterwards, all bets would be off. Denton would lock her in a tower with a medical warden to subdue her vibrant personality.

Turning her head, Claudia gave the papers a slow once over. Trace wanted to snatch them up, afraid this was all that remained of his time with Tori. She pointed to the picture on the brochure where Tori had highlighted all the names.

"I can't wait to see this place."

Trace frowned. "What is it?" Of all the places they'd checked for Tori, none of them had a sculpted palm garden shown in the picture.

"It's the Gardens at Currey Cove. Peter got hired on as a temp worker. He's already been over once today. He got me a spot serving drinks to some rich muckety-mucks."

Trace grabbed Claudia up in his arms and gave her a big, loud kiss on the cheek. Claudia's spine stiffened, and then her eyes rounded in shock. She stared at him with her mouth ajar.

"What did I say, so I can remember to repeat it everyday of my life?" she asked on a breathy whisper.

Trace laughed and released the woman he considered a friend. She'd welcomed Tori into the fold and she'd just given him the break he needed to find her. "Claudia, I need a favor."

"Anything, sugar," she said, patting the cheek he'd kissed.

"Call your man, Peter and have him give the minister a heads up. If he's a local bubba, he'll know what to do and when."

Turning to his crew, he said, "Let's go. I know where Tori is," Trace was already heading for the door.

✣

Tori stood at the altar. Built as a luxury getaway, Currey Cove had a resort style design with a single multiplex building that housed check-in, the restaurant, a spa and salon, a small gift shop, and a grand dining room. Tall candelabras stood like illuminated soldiers along the walls. A medium height gentleman wearing a black suit and a priest collar stood erect under a green vine covered trellis with giant floral swags. Denton had one of his henchmen drag her down the aisle. If any of his guests noticed how upset the bride appeared or the number of men on security detail, no one let on. The President's secret service detail had more gaps than the guys patrolling the perimeter. Denton stood beside her. When she would have stepped away to put additional space between them, he gripped her arm. His hold strangled her flesh, and she grit her teeth against the pain.

"Give me any trouble and I'll put your father to sleep permanently when I find him."

Hope, small by brilliant, burst forth in her heart. It had to be Trace. He had moved her father to protect him from Denton's reach. A small smile crossed her lips.

"That's more like it."

She glared at Denton. "Get over yourself. I'd prefer a drug-induced coma to you."

"I'm glad you're giddy about the future I have planned for you."

A shiver ran down her spine. Tori would not cry. Her father was safe, he was the last of her family...and Trace.

"Ladies and Gentlemen, we are gathered here today—"

The lights flickered off, and then on. Tori stiffened, and Denton noticed. With a slight tilt of his head, two of his henchman disappeared out of a side door. He shoved her forward.

"Finish this," he growled at the minister.

Tori heard a grunt before the room was plunged into darkness. The candelabras cast the room in shadows, but the space was too voluminous to see well in the low light. Murmurs came from the chairs behind her. A nervous Tori went to turn around, but Denton pulled her up to his side. The distinct muzzle of a gun was rammed into her side. Wincing, she jerked away from the pain.

Sudden panic swelled in her chest, but Tori pushed the emotion aside. She thought of her previous escape, reminded herself that this could be her opportunity to secure her freedom, once and for all. She needed to focus. Trace would come for her. She felt that truth with ever beat of her heart, now she needed to ensure she was ready to act when the moment arrived.

The minister's eyes widened, and then narrowed.

"Pronounce us man and wife," Denton demanded.

The middle-aged, slight framed gentleman straightened, his eyes hard and condemning. "I will not," he said, with a lift of his chin.

Denton smiled and pointed the gun at the clergy. "What about now? Does the 'good book' offer to you a solution to having your head blown off?"

Denton grinned, but there was no humor in the diabolical cackle.

The minister dropped his head in defeat. Tori gripped the veil that flowed the length of her body in both hands. As the man of God began to speak, Tori prayed. Was she truly marrying Denton? Grief flooded her, threatening to collapse her under its weight.

"Out of the depth of God's word," the official continued. Tori's fingers dug into the material bunched in her hands until the material ripped, and then she heard a distinct click. Heart thudding in her chest, her eyes shot to the altar and froze. Dear heaven—the minister had a gun trained on Denton. It was a smaller gun, maybe a Ruger LC9 or a Mustang.

"What the..." Denton shouted.

The wedding crowd erupted into chaos.

Now, a voice shouted in Tori's head. Without a second thought, she gathered her veil and flung the material at the flaming candles. Instantly the gauze caught fire.

Denton jumped back, temporarily freeing her arm.

"Run," the minister shouted without taking his eyes off Denton.

God's messenger spoke and the people listened. The cutting sound of heavy wood chairs scraping against hardwood floors filled the room. As people fled the scene, she could see Denton's guards losing the riot control battle with the scattering crowd.

Recognizing, this might be her one shot at seeing Trace again, Tori flung the blazing material in Denton's face. Seconds later, a fiery lash formed across his right jaw, his lips, and nose. The fatty stench of burning flesh soured the air and churned Tori's stomach. Denton roared in pain, the gun slipping from the hands scrambling to protect his now ruined face. How fitting that his scar would be more visible than hers.

"Princess!"

Tori's heart leaped in her chest. She began to turn in the direction of his voice. Trace had come for her.

"At the altar, Beastie," she projected her voice above the buzz of the runners and screamers. Energized, she wrestled to get the head dressing free of her ringlets.

Suddenly, a flash of heat singed her skin. Pain sliced through her arm. Denton held her left arm in a punishing grip.

"Even if you run, I'll still control fifty percent of the company," he bellowed. "You won't be free of me."

Tori didn't think, she pivoted and struck. She stomped on Denton's foot with her heel before jabbing him in the side. Stumbling backward, he released her. Running up the aisle, Tori didn't turn around when she heard Denton screaming after her.

Tori didn't stop running, not when the dress tangled under her feet, not when a powerful arm grabbed her waist and pulled her up short. She screamed and clawed.

"Let me go. Let me go," she pummeled the arm at her waist, as her feet flailed.

"Never letting you go, Princess."

"Trace?" The smoke had climber higher in the room making it more difficult to see.

"Yeah, it's me. We going to have a serious talk about the word, 'stay'."

She turned in his arms, snaking her arm around his neck. Trace stiffened in her arms. Before she could register what was happening, she was lifted off her feet and placed behind him.

Denton attacked Trace with a vengeance, his shoulder bull dozing into Trace's midsection. With one of his large hands, Trace pushed her out of the way.

"Stay back, Princess."

Trace's big body mowed down a few chairs as Denton continued his aggressive tackle. That's when Tori saw the syringe he held in his hand. She gasped. Denton was trying to kill him.

"Hasn't anyone told you that a commoner doesn't get the princess," Denton laughed, the sound maniacal.

Trace dodged when Denton swung, the syringe leading the way. But Denton's rage, must have multiplied his strength. They slipped and both went crashing to the floor, with Denton rolling over Trace. Dear heaven, Tori tried to scramble to Trace's aid. A blur flew through the air. Max bit into Denton's raised arm. He screamed. In an adept move, Trace twisted Denton's arm away from him. Grasping his hand, Trace drove the syringe into Denton's thigh, the pressure he applied to Denton's curled fingers depressing the plunger.

"No," Denton screamed before collapsing onto the floor.

"Guess no one told you, toads belong in the swamp."

Oxygen poured into her lungs, a fountain that fed her soul anew. "You saved me, again."

Trace turned to her, dark eyes gleaming. "Never losing you again, Tori. Marry me."

Suddenly, water rained down from the ceiling. The smoke must have triggered the built-in sprinklers. The downpour continued, the candles were extinguished, and darkness blanketed the room.

"What?" Tori couldn't believe what she was hearing. She was the impulsively cute one in the relationship. Marriage was a permanent commitment.

A hand landed on her bottom. "Woman, I want a yes, not another question. Do you love me enough to say, I do?"

Would he still want her after the adrenaline rush wore off? She was a tycoon's daughter that preferred wrecking balls to Wall Street. She had poor impulse control and a smart mouth.

"Ah," she hesitated. How often did that happen? The man she loved was offering forever and she was speechless.

Trace shrugged. "Whether you marry me or not, I'm still taking you home. You're brilliant and beautiful, and perfect. Just thought you'd want to scoop me up before word spread about what a great guy I am."

His tone said she'd be going home with him even if she thought to object. Which she wouldn't try with Trace.

Beams of joy filled her heart, and radiated from the depths of her soul. This was where she belonged. For the first time in her life, her square existence fit in the round hole of someone's life. Trace.

"You're such a salesman."

"Is it working?" he deadpanned.

"Yes. Yes, I want my Beastie forever."

❖

Lots of men and women in green uniforms with gold badges were entering the ballroom. Denton lay comatose on the floor and she was right where she wanted to be...in Trace's arms.

"Pretty dress, Princess."

"We are standing here in the dark, Trace?"

"So, we still have a few minutes before midnight."

"What about Denton?"

151

"Not trying to marry him."

She laughed. "He's still going to own part of the company."

"We'll deal with that when we get to it. You marry me, and your problems are solved. You get two for one. Firefighter by day, sex god at night."

She laughed. "That the only reason you're asking?"

"You want another spanking?"

She giggled. "Maybe, but..." she hesitated. "Do you want to marry me?"

"I asked, didn't I?"

"What about all the stuff you read to me in those books?"

"Romance?"

"Yes, and love."

"Oh," he grinned. "I'm all romance." He looked offended. "I'm the six pack of beer, box of candy hearts, and the Harlequin monthly subscription. It doesn't get more romantic than that."

She slapped his chest. He still hadn't said the he loved her.

"And," Trace said kissing her lips. "I'll love you until time runs out and starts over again. Now, it's an island and Lance has all the boats on lockdown. What do you say, Princess?"

"I say," she went up on tiptoe, placing a kiss on his lips. "I've been waiting for you my whole life. I love you too."

Trace howled. "Somebody turn on the lights and find that minister."

Tori's wedding day was filled with fire and rain, a villain, prince charming, and a daring rescue. She'd never been happier.

Chapter Thirteen

Now that Denton was behind bars and awaiting trial, Tori's life was pretty ordinary.

"How far apart are her contractions?" Tori asked Nathan as she regarded Symphony's exhausted face and rigid posture in the hospital bed.

Symphony had gone into labor at the wedding reception. She and Trace had been married for two days. They both wanted to have a ceremony where all their friends were present. So, forty-eight hours after she said I do with a charred veil on her head standing in a puddle of water, she and Trace renewed their vows. Her father had walked her down the aisle to her husband, and one of her friends from her Johns Hopkins days, Dr. Logan Masters had driven down for the wedding. Logan was a pediatric surgeon on staff at one of north Florida's leading medical centers. During his residency, he'd volunteered hundreds of hours with Tori's mom at the women's shelter. With his ruddy blond mane and vivid green eyes, the man should never be without a woman, yet he was always alone. Tori often wondered if Logan had his own story of betrayal. How tragic she thought because she'd had never been happier.

"Don't know. I'm not a paramedic right now, Tori. I'm a soon to be father," Nathan grumbled.

Apparently, her father's mental state had improved significantly since he'd stopped taking all the medications provided by Denton's physician. Tori learned her father hadn't abandoned her to Denton's mercy. While she'd been taken hostage, he'd telephoned his lawyer and revoked the stipulations of her trust and fired Denton.

Strong arms slid around her waist. "You okay, Princess?"

"Never better." She smiled up at her husband's handsome face, settling into the loving heat of his warrior's body.

She touched the rose pendant dangling from the chain around her neck. Trace had made a call, and poof, her beloved heirloom had arrived by courier the next day. Trace had fumbled with the tiny clasp, followed by a string of profanity, as he locked it around her neck.

Ten hours later Lyric Axyla Zachary was in her mother's arms. Tori laughed as three huge men, oohed and aahed over the little girl with her father's raven black waves and her mother's golden amber eyes. A soft gurgle came from tiny lips and the adults in the room erupted in cheers. Bliss and absolute joy was a tangible presence in the room. There were 'first female president' predictions followed by Supreme Court justice appointments. The baby was beautiful and Tori ran a hand over her belly. Did Trace want children?

Nathan sat in the reclining chair at his wife's bedside. With his infant daughter cradled in one arm, he held his wife's hand while she slept. Tears sprang to Tori's eyes. She thought Denton's actions had damaged her in some irreparable way. No, she was stronger now than she'd ever been. Trace's love had shown her she was flawed, like him, but not broken. His acceptance and complete devotion had won her heart.

"How many kids do you want, Princess?" Trace asked, with her across his lap.

"As many as you'll give me."

He chuckled and placed a kiss on her cheek. "I love you, Mrs. Fletcher."

"I love you more," she teased.

"You can prove it in bed, tonight. I have every intention of exploring your assets."

"You're so raunchy, but I have an extensive portfolio that's worth a thorough once over."

"Yeah, and your man is proud of how you manage it," Trace murmured.

Cutler groaned. "Man, cut it out. You know I'm not getting any action."

Tori looked over just in time to see Kendall elbowing her fiancé in the ribs.

"You get plenty of action."

Cutler scoffed. "Her grandmother recommended a pre-martial counselor that touts abstinence before marriage."

"Ah, poor baby," Kendall said, patting his head.

"Keep messing around. We gonna need counseling to recover from the counseling," Cutler said, before breaking into a laugh.

"When's the wedding?" Tori asked.

Kendall smiled down at her island cowboy. "As soon as Trace's temporary replacement comes on board we are headed to Vegas for two weeks."

"Wow," Tori said.

"Nope," Trace said, coming to his feet with her in his arms. "We are not having a third ceremony. You're mine, twice over."

"Oh, come on. Let's do the Vegas Elvis thing at

one of the resorts on The Strip, maybe Camelot or Excalibur." Tori clapped her hands in excitement.

"Oh, I've got some medieval shit planned for you right here in Key West, and then again in Dallas."

She smiled looking forward to her next adventure with her Trace, her dream lover.

"Who's coming from DF&R 58?" Trace asked.

"I have my suspicions," Kendall said, her voice dreamy.

"Must be gorgeous," Tori chimed in.

"If it's who I think, his name and the body are a matched set. Throw in his Harley and the man practically owns every pair of panties when he walks in the place," Kendall squealed.

"He better not have any damn panties from the three of you." Nathan rose from the chair, but stayed at his wife's side.

Tori had a home in Trace's heart and with her new friends. As she regarded each face in the room, she remembered a few days ago she thought she was all alone in the world. How wrong she had been. The only impulse she felt in that moment was to dig in her heels and hold onto her happily ever after. That empty place in her heart softened, a sprout of green peeked through the soil fertilized with love. She had the man who filled her dreams with storybook magic and her heart with love. As if the moment was to sacred, little Lyric Axyla decided to raise the short hairs on everyone's neck by unleashing a glass-shattering howl.

Trace leaned forward and whispered in her ear. "You sure you want one?"

"To quote my poetic husband, 'among other things'." Tori turned to kiss her husband. Indeed, everything was coming up roses.

❖

If you loved Trace and Victoria's story, download Nathan and Symphony's story
In
CHASING FLAMES

And

Cutler and Kendall's story
In
CONCEALING FIRE

✤

Siera London is a Bestselling Author of contemporary romance and romantic suspense. She crafts stories of diverse characters navigating the challenges and triumphs to find lasting love. Intelligence, wit, emotion, drama, and sensual romance are between the covers of every Siera London novel.

Follow Siera and learn more about her books:

Amazon http://amzn.to/1Oce1Ht

BookBub: https://www.bookbub.com/authors/siera-london

Like Siera London Books Facebook page https://www.facebook.com/authorsieralondon/

Instagram· https://www.instagram.com/sieralondon

Twitter www.twitter.com/siera_london

Pinterest: https://www.pinterest.com/sieralondon

Goodreads: https://www.goodreads.com/siera_london

To stay in touch sign up for my newsletter here:
http://eepurl.com/bE-Lof

You can find more information about Paige Tyler's Dallas Fire and Rescue here: http://paigetylertheauthor.com/BooksDallasFireAndRescueKind.

<<<<>>>>

Made in the USA
San Bernardino, CA
20 April 2018